HORRiD HENRY'S
Tricky Tricks

Francesca Simon

HORRiD HENRY'S Tricky Tricks

Illustrated by Tony Ross

Orion
Children's Books

This collection first published in Great Britain in 2014
by Orion Children's Books
a division of the Orion Publishing Group Ltd
Orion House
5 Upper St Martin's Lane
London WC2H 9EA
An Hachette UK Company

1 3 5 7 9 10 8 6 4 2

ISBN 978 1 4440 1208 8

Printed in China

www.orionbooks.co.uk
www.horridhenry.co.uk

Contents

Prepare to be tricked, you wormy worms!

Weepy William

Mrs Oddbod

Bossy Bill

Mum

Dad

Perfect Peter

Miss Battle-Axe

Moody Margaret

Sour Susan

HORRID HENRY
Robs the Bank

'**I** want the skull!'

'I want the skull!'

'*I* want the skull!' said Horrid Henry, glaring.

'You had it last time, Henry,' said Perfect Peter. 'I *never* get it.'

'Did not.'

'Did too.'

'*I'm* the guest so *I* get the skull,' said Moody Margaret, snatching it from the box. '*You* can have the claw.'

'NOOOOOOOO!' wailed Henry. 'The skull is my lucky piece.'

Margaret looked smug. 'You know I'm going to win, Henry, 'cause I always do. So ha ha ha.'

'Wanna bet?' muttered Horrid Henry.

The good news was that Horrid Henry was playing *Gotcha*, the world's best board game. Horrid Henry loved *Gotcha*. You rolled the dice and travelled round the board, collecting treasure, buying dragon lairs and praying you didn't land in your enemies' lairs or in the Dungeon.

The bad news was that Horrid Henry was having to play *Gotcha* with his worm toad crybaby brother.

The worst news was that Moody Margaret, the world's biggest cheater, was playing with them.

Margaret's mum was out for the afternoon, and had dumped Margaret at Henry's. Why oh why did she have to play at his house? Why couldn't her mum just dump her in the bin where she belonged?

Unfortunately, the last time they'd played *Gotcha*, Margaret had won. The last two, three, four and five times they'd played, Margaret had won. Margaret was a demon *Gotcha* player.

Well, not any longer.

This time, Henry was determined to beat her. Horrid Henry hated losing. By hook or by crook, he would triumph. Moody Margaret had beaten him at *Gotcha* for the very last time.

'Who'll be banker?' said Perfect Peter.

'Me,' said Margaret.

'Me,' said Henry. Being in charge of all the game's treasure was an excellent way of topping up your coffers when none of the other players was looking.

'I'm the guest so *I'm* banker,' said Margaret. 'You can be the dragon keeper.'

Horrid Henry's hand itched to yank Margaret's hair. But then Margaret would scream and scream and Mum would send Henry to his room and confiscate *Gotcha* until Henry was old and bald and dead.

'Touch any treasure that isn't yours, and you're dragon food,' hissed Henry.

'Steal any dragon eggs that aren't yours and you're toast,' hissed Margaret.

'If you're banker and Henry's the dragon keeper, what am I?' said Perfect Peter.

'A toad,' said Henry. 'And count yourself lucky.'

Horrid Henry snatched the dice. 'I'll go first.' The player who went first always had the best chance of buying up the best dragon lairs like Eerie Eyrie and Hideous Hellmouth.

'No,' said Margaret, 'I'll go first.'

'I'm the youngest, I should go first,' said Peter.

'Me!' said Margaret, snatching the dice. 'I'm the guest.'

'Me!' said Henry, snatching them back.

'Me!' said Peter.

'MUM!' screamed Henry and Peter.

Mum ran in. 'You haven't even started playing and already you're fighting,' said Mum.

'It's my turn to go first!' wailed Henry, Margaret, and Peter.

'The rules say to roll the dice and whoever gets the highest number goes first,' said Mum. 'End of story.' She left, closing the door behind her.

Henry rolled. Four. Not good.

'Peter's knee touched mine when I rolled the dice,' protested Henry. 'I get another turn.'

'No you don't,' said Margaret.

'Muuum! Henry's cheating!' shrieked Peter.

'If I get called one more time,' screamed Mum from upstairs, 'I will throw that game in the bin.'

Eeeek.

Margaret rolled. Three.

'You breathed on me,' hissed Margaret.

'Did not,' said Henry.

'Did too,' said Margaret. 'I get another go.'

'No way,' said Henry.

Peter picked up the dice.

'Low roll, low roll, low roll,' chanted Henry.

'Stop it, Henry,' said Peter.

'Low roll, low roll, low roll,' chanted Henry louder.

Peter rolled an eleven.

'Yippee, I go first,' trilled Peter.

Henry glared at him.

Perfect Peter took a deep breath, and rolled the dice to start the game.

Five. A Fate square.

Perfect Peter moved his gargoyle to the Fate square and picked up a Fate card. Would it tell him to claim a treasure hoard, or send him to the Dungeon? He squinted at it.

'The og . . . the ogr . . . I can't read it,' he said. 'The words are too hard for me.'

Henry snatched the card. It read:

The Ogres make you king for a day. Collect 20 rubies from the other players.

'The Ogres make you king for a day. Give 20 rubies to the player on your left,' read Henry. 'And that's me, so pay up.'

Perfect Peter handed Henry twenty rubies.

Tee hee, thought Horrid Henry.

'I think you read that Fate card wrong, Henry,' said Moody Margaret grimly.

Uh oh. If Margaret read Peter the card, he was dead. Mum would make them stop playing, and Henry would get into trouble. Big, big trouble.

'Didn't,' said Henry.

'Did,' said Margaret. 'I'm telling on you.'

Horrid Henry looked at the card again. 'Whoops. Silly me. I read it too fast,' said Henry. 'It says, give 20 rubies to *all* the other players.'

'Thought so,' said Moody Margaret.

Perfect Peter rolled the dice. Nine! Oh no, that took Peter straight to Eerie Eyrie, Henry's favourite lair. Now Peter could buy it. Everyone always landed on it and had to pay ransom or get eaten. Rats, rats, rats.

'1, 2, 3, 4, 5, 6, 7, 8, 9, look, Henry, I've landed on Eerie Eyrie and no one owns it yet,' said Peter.

'Don't buy it,' said Henry. 'It's the worst lair on the board. No one ever lands on it. You'd just be wasting your money.'

'Oh,' said Peter. He looked doubtful.

'But . . . but . . .' said Peter.

'Save your money for when you land in other people's lairs,' said Henry. 'That's what I'd do.'

'OK,' said Peter, 'I'm not buying.'

Tee hee.

Henry rolled. Six. Yes! He landed on Eerie Eyrie. 'I'm buying it!' crowed Henry.

'But Henry,' said Peter, 'you just told me not to buy it.'

'You shouldn't listen to me,' said Henry.

'MUM!' wailed Peter.

Soon Henry owned Eerie Eyrie, Gryphon Gulch and Creepy Hollow, but he was dangerously low on treasure. Margaret owned Rocky Ravine, Vulture Valley, and Hideous Hellmouth. Margaret kept her treasure in her treasure pouch, so it was impossible to see how much money she had, but Henry guessed she was also low.

Peter owned Demon Den and one dragon egg.

Margaret was stuck in the Dungeon. Yippee! This meant if Henry landed on one of her lairs he'd be safe. Horrid Henry rolled, and landed on Vulture Valley, guarded by a baby dragon.

'Gotcha!' shrieked Margaret. 'Gimme 25 rubies.'

'You're in the Dungeon, you can't collect ransom,' said Henry. 'Nah nah ne nah nah!'

'Can!'

'Can't!'

'That's how we play in *my* house,' said Margaret.

'In case you hadn't noticed, we're not *at* your house,' said Henry.

'But I'm the guest,' said Margaret. 'Gimme my money!'

'No!' shouted Henry. 'You can't just make up rules.'

'The rules say . . .' began Perfect Peter.

'Shut up, Peter!' screamed Henry and Margaret.

'I'm not paying,' said Henry.

Margaret glowered. 'I'll get you for this, Henry,' she hissed.

It was Peter's turn. Henry had just upgraded his baby dragon guarding Eerie Eyrie to a big, huge, fire-breathing, slavering monster dragon. Peter was only five squares away. If Peter landed there, he'd be out of the game.

'Land! Land! Land! Land! Land!' chanted Henry. 'Yum yum yum, my dragon is just waiting to eat you up.'

'Stop it, Henry,' said Peter. He rolled. Five.

'Gotcha!' shouted Horrid Henry. 'I own Eerie Eyrie! You've landed in my lair, pay up! That's 100 rubies.'

'I don't have enough money,' wailed Perfect Peter.

Horrid Henry drew his finger across his throat.

'You're dead meat, worm,' he chortled.

Perfect Peter burst into tears and ran out of the room.

'Waaaaaaahhhhh,' he wailed. 'I lost!'

Horrid Henry glared at Moody Margaret.

Moody Margaret glared at Horrid Henry.

'You're next to be eaten,' snarled Margaret.

'*You're* next,' snarled Henry.

Henry peeked under the *Gotcha* board where his
treasure was hidden. Oh no. Not again. He'd spent so
much on dragons he was down to his last few rubies.
If he landed on any of Margaret's lairs, he'd be wiped
out. He had to get more treasure. He had to. Why
oh why had he let Margaret be banker?

His situation was desperate. Peter was easy to steal
money from, but Margaret's eagle eyes never missed
a trick. What to do, what to do? He had to get more
treasure, he had to.

And then suddenly Horrid Henry had a brilliant,
spectacular idea. It was so brilliant that Henry couldn't
believe he'd never thought of it before. It was
dangerous. It was risky. But what choice did he have?

'I need the loo,' said Henry.

'Hurry up,' said Margaret, scowling.

Horrid Henry dashed to the downstairs loo . . .
and sneaked straight out of the back door. Then

21

he jumped over the garden wall and crept into
Margaret's house.

Quickly he ran to her sitting room and scanned
her games cupboard. Aha! There was Margaret's
Gotcha.

Horrid Henry stuffed his pockets with treasure. He
stuffed more under his shirt and in his socks.

'Is that you, my little sugarplum?' came a voice
from upstairs. 'Maggie Moo-Moo?'

Henry froze. Margaret's mum was home.

'Maggie Plumpykins,' cooed her mum, coming
down the stairs. 'Is that you–oooo?'

'No,' squeaked Henry. 'I mean, yes,' he squawked. 'Got to go back to Henry's, 'bye!'

And Horrid Henry ran for his life.

'You took a long time,' said Margaret.

Henry hugged his stomach.

'Upset tummy,' he lied. Oh boy was he brilliant. Now, with loads of cash which he would slip under the board, he was sure to win.

Henry picked up the dice and handed them to Margaret.

'Your turn,' said Henry.

Henry's hungry dragon stood waiting six places away in Goblin Gorge.

Roll a six, roll a six, roll a six, prayed Horrid Henry.

Not a six, not a six, not a six, prayed Moody Margaret.

Margaret rolled. Four. She moved her skull to the Haunted Forest.

'Your turn,' said Margaret.

Henry rolled a three. Oh no. He'd landed on Hideous Hellmouth, where Margaret's giant dragon loomed.

'Yes!' squealed Margaret. 'Gotcha! You're dead! Ha ha hahaha, I won!' Moody Margaret leapt to her feet and did a victory dance, whooping and cheering.

Horrid Henry smiled at her.

'Oh dear,' said Horrid Henry. 'Oh dearie, dearie me. Looks like I'm dragon food – NOT!'

'What do you mean, not?' said Margaret. 'You're dead meat, you can't pay me.'

'Not so fast,' said Horrid Henry. With a flourish he reached under the board and pulled out a wodge of treasure.

'Let me see, 100 rubies, is it?' said Henry, counting off a pile of coins.

Margaret's mouth dropped open.

'How did you . . . what . . . how . . . huh?' she spluttered.

Henry shrugged modestly. 'Some of us know how to play this game,' he said. 'Now roll.'

Moody Margaret rolled and landed on a Fate square.

Go straight to Eerie Eyrie, read the card.

'Gotcha!' shrieked Horrid Henry. He'd won!! Margaret didn't have enough money to stop being eaten. She was dead. She was doomed.

'I won! I won! You can't pay me, nah nah ne nah nah,' shrieked Horrid Henry, leaping up and doing a victory dance. 'I am the *Gotcha* king!'

'Says who?' said Moody Margaret, pulling a handful of treasure from her pouch.

Huh?

'You stole that money!' spluttered Henry. 'You stole the bank's money. You big fat cheater.'

'Didn't.'

'Did.'

'CHEATER!' howled Moody Margaret.

'CHEATER!' howled Horrid Henry.

Moody Margaret grabbed the board and hurled it to the floor.

'I won,' said Horrid Henry.

'Did not.'

'Did too, Maggie Moo-Moo.'

'Don't call me that,' said Margaret, glaring.

'Call you what, Moo-Moo?'

'I challenge you to a re-match,' said Moody Margaret.

'You're on,' said Horrid Henry.

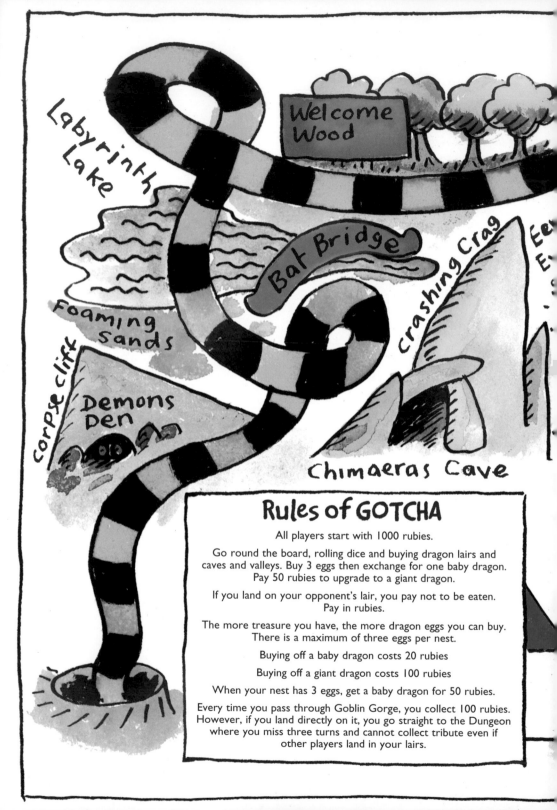

Labyrinth Lake

Welcome Wood

Bat Bridge

Crashing Crag

Ee
E
S

Foaming sands

Corpse cliff

Demons Den

Chimaeras Cave

Rules of GOTCHA

All players start with 1000 rubies.

Go round the board, rolling dice and buying dragon lairs and caves and valleys. Buy 3 eggs then exchange for one baby dragon. Pay 50 rubies to upgrade to a giant dragon.

If you land on your opponent's lair, you pay not to be eaten. Pay in rubies.

The more treasure you have, the more dragon eggs you can buy. There is a maximum of three eggs per nest.

Buying off a baby dragon costs 20 rubies

Buying off a giant dragon costs 100 rubies

When your nest has 3 eggs, get a baby dragon for 50 rubies.

Every time you pass through Goblin Gorge, you collect 100 rubies. However, if you land directly on it, you go straight to the Dungeon where you miss three turns and cannot collect tribute even if other players land in your lairs.

Hideous Hellmouth

Gryphon
Gulch

Vulture Valley

Rocky Ravine

Terror
Tower

Robbers
Roadblock
Pay
Treasury
1 Ruby

Gnashers Gorge

tal
n

gey bluff

Blustery
Brambles

FLUFFY
Struts Her Stuff

'**F**luffy. Fetch,' said Perfect Peter.

Snore.

'Fluffy. Fetch!' said Perfect Peter.

Snore.

'Go on, Fluffy,' said Perfect Peter, dangling a squeaky toy tarantula in front of the snoozing cat. 'Fetch!'

Fat Fluffy stretched.

Yawn.

Snore. Snore.

'What *are* you doing, worm?' said Horrid Henry.

Peter jumped. Should he tell Henry about his brilliant idea? What if Henry copied him? That would be just like Henry. Well, let him try, thought Peter. Fluffy is my cat.

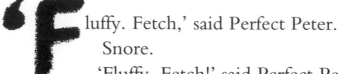

'I'm training Fluffy for Scruffs,' said Peter. 'She's sure to win this year.'

Scruffs was the annual neighbourhood pet show. Last year Henry had spent one of the most boring days of his life watching horrible dogs compete for who looked the most like their owner, or who had the waggiest tail or fluffiest coat.

32

Horrid Henry snorted.

'Which category?' said Henry. 'Ugliest Owner? Fattest Cat?'

'*Most Obedient,*' said Peter.

Horrid Henry snorted again. Trust his worm toad nappy face brother to come up with such a dumb idea.

Fat Fluffy was the world's most useless cat. Fluffy did nothing but eat and sleep and snore. She was so lazy that Horrid Henry was shocked every time she moved.

Squeak! Perfect Peter waved the rubber tarantula in front of Fluffy's face. He knew Henry would make fun of him. Well, this time he, Peter, would have the last laugh. He would show the world what an amazing cat Fluffy was, and no one, especially Henry, could stop him. Peter knew that

33

Fluffy had hidden greatness. After all, thought Peter, not everyone knows how clever *I* am. The same was true of Fluffy.

'Fluffy, when I squeak this toy, you sit up and give me your paw,' said Peter. 'When I squeak it twice, you roll over.'

'You can't train a cat, toad,' said Henry.

'Yes I can,' said Peter. 'And don't call me toad.' What did Henry know, anyway? Nothing. Peter had seen dogs herding sheep. Jumping through hoops. Even dancing.

True, they had all been dogs, and Fluffy was a cat. But she was no ordinary cat.

Horrid Henry smirked.

'Okay Peter, because I'm such a nice brother I'll show you how to train Fluffy,' said Henry.

'Can you really?' said Peter.

'Yup,' said Henry. 'When I give the command, Fluffy will do exactly what I say.'

So far that was more than Peter had managed. A lot more.

'And it will only cost you £1,' said Henry.

Well, it was definitely worth a pound if it meant Fluffy could win Most Obedient.

Peter handed over the money.

'Now watch and learn, worm,' said Horrid Henry.

'Fluffy. Sleep!'

Fluffy slept.

'See?' said Henry. 'She obeyed.'

Perfect Peter was outraged.

'That doesn't count,' said Peter. 'I want my money back.'

'You can't have it,' said Henry. 'I did exactly what I said I would do.'

'Mum!' wailed Peter. 'Henry tricked me.'

'Shut up, toad,' said Horrid Henry.

'Mum! Henry told me to shut up,' screamed Peter.

'Henry! Don't be horrid,' shouted Mum.

Horrid Henry wasn't listening. He was an idiot. He had just had the most brilliant, spectacular idea. He could train Fluffy *and* play the best ever trick on Peter in the history of the world. No, the universe. That would pay Peter back for getting Henry into such big trouble over breaking Mum's camera. One day, thought Horrid Henry, he would write a famous book collecting all his best tricks, and sell it for a

million pounds a copy. Parliament would declare
a special holiday – *Henry Day* – to celebrate his
brilliance. There would be street parties and parades
in his honour. The Queen would knight him. But
until then . . . he had work to do.

Horrid Henry gave Peter back his £1 coin.

Perfect Peter was amazed. Henry never handed
back money voluntarily. He looked at the coin
suspiciously. Had Henry substituted a plastic pound
coin like the last time?

'That was just a joke,' said Henry smoothly. 'Of
course I can train Fluffy for you.'

'How?' said Peter. He'd been trying for days.

'That's my secret,' said Henry. 'But I am so confident I can do it I'll even give you a money-back guarantee.'

A money-back guarantee! That sounded almost too good to be true. In fact . . .

'Is this a trick?' said Peter.

'No!' said Henry. 'Out of the goodness of my heart, I offer to spend my valuable time training your cat. I'm insulted. Just for that I won't—'

'Okay,' said Peter. 'How much?'

Yes! thought Horrid Henry.

'£5,' said Henry.

'£5!' gasped Peter.

'That's a bargain,' said Henry, 'Not everyone can train a cat. Okay, £5 money-back guarantee that Fluffy will obey four commands in time for Scruffs. If not, you'll get your money back.'

How could he lose? thought Peter. 'Deal,' he said.

Yes! thought Horrid Henry.

Somehow he didn't think he'd have too much trouble training Fluffy to Stay. Sleep. Breathe. Snore. No trouble at all.

Perfect Peter bounced up and down with excitement. Today was the big day. Today was the day when he took Fluffy to win Most Obedient pet at Scruffs.

'Shouldn't I practise with her?' said Peter.

'No!' said Henry quickly. 'Cats are tricky. You only get one chance to make them obey, so we need to save it for the judge.'

'Okay, Henry,' said Peter. After all, Henry had given him a money-back guarantee.

Greedy Graham was at the park with his enormous guinea pig, Fattie. Rude Ralph had brought his mutt, Windbag, who was competing for Waggiest Tail.
Sour Susan was there with her pug, Grumpy. Aerobic Al was there with his greyhound, Speedy. Lazy Linda's

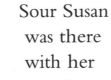

rabbit, Snore, dozed on her shoulder. Even Miss Lovely had brought her Yorkie, Baby Jane. There were pets everywhere.

'What's your dog called, Bert?' said Henry.

'I dunno,' said Beefy Bert.

'Waaah,' wailed Weepy William. 'Mr Socks didn't win the Fluffiest Kitty contest.'

'Piddle. Sit!' came a familiar, steely voice, like a jagged knife being dragged across a boulder.

Horrid Henry gasped.

There was Miss Battle-Axe, walking beside the most groomed dog Henry had ever seen. The poodle was covered in ribbons and fancy collars and velvet bows.

He watched as Miss Battle-Axe found a quiet corner and put on some music.

Boom-chick boom-chick boom-chick-boom!

Miss Battle-Axe danced around Piddle.

She clicked her fingers.

Piddle danced around Miss Battle-Axe.

Miss Battle-Axe danced backwards, waving her arms and clicking again.

Piddle danced backwards.

Miss Battle-Axe danced forwards, hopping. Piddle danced forwards.

Double click. Miss Battle-Axe danced off to the left. Piddle danced off to the right. Then they met back at the centre.

Finally, Miss Battle-Axe crouched, and Piddle jumped over her.

'Wow,' said Perfect Peter, glancing at Fat Fluffy snoring on the grass. 'Do you think we could teach Fluffy to do tricks like that?'

'Already have,' said Horrid Henry.

Peter gazed at Henry open-mouthed.

'Really?' said Peter.

'Yup,' said Henry. 'Just squeeze the tarantula and tell Fluffy what you want her to do.'

'Line up here for Most Obedient pet,' said the organiser.

'That's me!' said Peter.

'All you have to remember, one squeak to make Fluffy sit up, two squeaks to make her walk on her hind legs,' said Henry as they stood in the queue. 'Three squeaks will make her come running to you.'

'Okay, Henry,' said Peter.

Tee hee.

Revenge was sweet, thought Horrid Henry. Wouldn't Peter look an idiot trying to give orders to a cat? And naturally he'd find a way to keep Peter's £5.

Peter handed in his entry ticket at the enclosure's entrance.

'Sorry, your brother's too young,' said the man at the gate. 'You'll have to show the cat.'

Horrid Henry froze with horror.

'Me?' said Horrid Henry. 'But . . . but . . .'

'But she's my cat,' said Perfect Peter. 'I—'

'Come along, come along, we're about to start,'

said the man, shoving Henry and Fat Fluffy into the ring.

Horrid Henry found himself standing in the centre. He had the only cat. Everyone was staring and pointing and laughing. Oh, where was a cloak of invisibility when you needed one?

'Put your pets through their paces now,' shouted the judge.

All the dogs started to Sit. Stay. Come. Fetch. Piddle the poodle began to dance.

Fluffy lay curled in a ball at Henry's feet.

'Stay!' said

Horrid Henry as the judge walked by.

Maybe he could get Fluffy at least to sit up. Or even just move a bit.

Horrid Henry squeezed the tarantula toy.

Squeak!

'Come on, Fluffy. Move!'

Fluffy didn't even raise her head.

Squeak! Squeak! Squeak!

'Fluffy. Wake up!'

Aerobic Al's dog began to bark.

Horrid Henry squeezed the tarantula toy again.

Squeak! Squeak!

Piddle stood on his hind legs and danced in a circle.

'No, Piddle,' hissed Miss Battle-Axe, gesturing wildly, 'turn to the right.'

'Fluffy. Sit!' said Horrid Henry.

Squeak! Squeak!

Babbling Bob's mutt started growling.

Come on, Fluffy, thought Horrid Henry desperately, squeezing the toy in front of the dozing cat. 'Do something. Anything.'

Squeeeeak.
Squeeeeeeak!
Squeeeeeeeeeeak!

Piddle ran over and peed on the judge's leg.

'Piddle,' squawked Miss Battle-Axe. 'NO!'

Squeak!
Squeak!
Squeak!

Sour Susan's dog

Grumpy bit the dog next to him.

Horrid Henry waved his arms. 'Come on, Fluffy. You can do it!'

Weepy William's dog started running in circles.

'Piddle! Come back!' shrieked Miss Battle-Axe as Piddle ran from the ring, howling. Every other dog chased after him, barking and yelping, their owners running after them screaming.

The only animal left was Fat Fluffy.

'Fluffy. Stay!' ordered Horrid Henry.

Snore. Snore. Snore.

'The cat's the winner,' said the judge.

'Yippee!' screamed Perfect Peter. 'I knew you could do it, Fluffy!'

'Meow.'

Pets and their owners

Rude Ralph and Windbag

Greedy Graham and guinea pig, Fattie

Sour Susan with pug, Grumpy

Stuck-up Steve with Snooty the Schnauzer

Aerobic Al and Speedy the greyhound

Miss Lovely and yorkie, Baby Jane

weepy William and
kitten, Socks

Lazy Linda's rabbit, Snore

Miss Battle-Axe and
Piddle the Poodle

Mr Mossy and his baldy dog

Great Aunt Greta and
her cat, Boney

Vomiting Vera and
puppy, upchuck

HORRID HENRY
Wakes the Dead

'**N**o, no, no, no, no!' shouted Miss Battle-Axe. 'Spitting is not a talent, Graham. Violet, you can't do the can-can as your talent. Ralph, burping to the beat is not a talent.'

She turned to Bert. 'What's your talent?'

'I dunno,' said Beefy Bert.

'And what about you, Steven?' said Miss Battle-Axe grimly.

'Caveman,' grunted Stone-Age Steven. 'Ugg!'

Horrid Henry had had enough.

'Me next!' shrieked Horrid Henry. 'I've got a great talent! Me next!'

'Me!' shrieked Moody Margaret.

'Me!' shrieked Rude Ralph.

'No one who shouts out will be performing *anything*,' said Miss Battle-Axe.

Next week was Horrid Henry's school talent show. But this wasn't an ordinary school talent show. Oh no. This year was different. This year, the famous TV presenter Sneering Simone was choosing the winner.

But best and most fantastic of all, the prize was a chance to appear on Simone's TV programme *Talent Tigers*. And from there . . . well, there was no end to the fame and fortune which awaited the winner.

Horrid Henry had to win. He just had to. A chance to be on TV! A chance for his genius to be recognised, at last.

The only problem was, he had so many talents it was impossible to pick just one. He could eat crisps faster than Greedy Graham. He could burp to the theme tune of *Marvin the Maniac*.

He could stick out his tongue almost as far as Moody Margaret.

But brilliant as these talents were, perhaps they weren't *quite* special enough to win. Hmmmm . . .

Wait, he had it.

He could perform his new rap, 'I have an ugly brother, ick ick ick/ A smelly toad brother, who makes me sick.' That would be sure to get him on *Talent Tigers*.

'Margaret!' barked Miss Battle-Axe, 'what's your talent?'

'Susan and I are doing a rap,' said Moody Margaret.

What?

'*I'm* doing a rap,' howled Henry. How dare Margaret steal his idea!

'Only one person can do a rap,' said Miss Battle-Axe firmly.

'Unfair!' shrieked Horrid Henry.

'Be quiet, Henry,' said Miss Battle-Axe.

Moody Margaret stuck out her tongue at Horrid Henry. 'Nah nah ne nah nah.'

Horrid Henry stuck out his tongue at Moody Margaret. Aaaarrgh! It was so unfair.

'I'm doing a hundred push-ups,' said Aerobic Al.

'I'm playing the drums,' said Jazzy Jim.

'I want to do a rap!' howled Horrid Henry. 'Mine's much better than hers!'

'You have to do something else or not take part,' said Miss Battle-Axe, consulting her list.

Not take part? Was Miss Battle-Axe out of her mind? Had all those years working on a chain gang done her in?

Miss Battle-Axe stood in front of Henry, baring her fangs. Her pen tapped impatiently on her notebook.

'Last chance, Henry. List closes in ten seconds . . .'

What to do, what to do?

'I'll do magic,' said Horrid Henry. How hard could it be to do some magic? He wasn't a master of disguise and the fearless leader of the Purple Hand Gang for nothing. In fact, not only would he do magic, he would do the greatest magic trick the world had ever seen. No rabbits out of a hat. No flowers out of a cane. No sawing a girl in half–though if Margaret volunteered Henry would be very happy to oblige.

No! He, Henry, Il Stupendioso, the greatest magician ever, would . . . would . . . he would wake the dead.

Wow. That was much cooler than a rap. He could see it now. He would chant his magic spells and wave his magic wand, until slowly, slowly, slowly, out of the coffin the bony body would rise, sending the audience screaming out of the hall!

Yes! thought Horrid Henry, *Talent Tigers* here I come. All he needed was an assistant.

Unfortunately, no one in his class wanted to assist him.

'Are you crazy?' said Gorgeous Gurinder.

'I've got a much better talent than *that*. No way,' said Clever Clare.

'Wake the dead?' gasped Weepy William. 'Nooooo.'

Rats, thought Horrid Henry. For his spectacular trick to work, an assistant was essential. Henry hated working with other children, but sometimes it couldn't be helped. Was there anyone he knew who would do exactly as they were told? Someone who would obey his every order? Hmmm. Perhaps there was a certain someone who would even pay for the privilege of being in his show.

Perfect Peter was busy emptying the dishwasher without being asked.

'Peter,' said Henry sweetly, 'how much would you pay me if I let you be in my magic show?'

Perfect Peter couldn't believe his ears. Henry was asking him to be in his show. Peter had always wanted to be in a show. And now Henry was actually asking him after he'd said no a million times. It was a dream come true. He'd pay anything.

'I've got £6.27 in my piggy bank,' said Peter eagerly.

Horrid Henry pretended to think.

'Done!' said Horrid Henry. 'You can start by painting the coffin black.'

'Thank you, Henry,' said Peter humbly, handing over the money.

Tee hee, thought Horrid Henry, pocketing the loot.

Henry told Peter what he had to do. Peter's jaw dropped.

'And will my name be on the billboard so everyone will know I'm your assistant?' asked Peter.

'Of course,' said Horrid Henry.

The great day arrived at last. Henry had practised and practised and practised. His magic robes were ready. His magic spells were ready. His coffin was ready. His props were ready. Even his dead body was as ready as it would ever be. Victory was his!

Henry and Peter stood backstage and peeked through the curtain as the audience charged into the hall. The school was buzzing. Parents pushed and shoved to get the best seats. There was a stir as Sneering Simone swept in, taking her seat in the front row.

'Would you *please* move?' demanded Margaret's mother, waving her camcorder. 'I can't see my little Maggie Muffin.'

'And I can't see Al with *your* big head in the way,' snapped Aerobic Al's dad, shoving his camera in front of Moody Margaret's mum.

'Parents, behave!' shouted Mrs Oddbod. 'What an exciting programme we have for you today! You will be amazed at all the talents in this school. First Clare will recite Pi, which as you all know is the ratio of the circumference of a circle to the diameter, to 31 significant figures!'

'3.14159 26535 89793 23846 26433 83279,' said Clever Clare.

Sneering Simone made a few notes.

'Boring,' shouted Horrid Henry. 'Boring!'

'Shhh,' hissed Miss Battle-Axe.

'Now, Gurinder, Linda, Fiona and Zoe proudly present: the cushion dance!'

Gorgeous Gurinder, Lazy Linda, Fiery Fiona and Zippy Zoe ran on stage and placed a cushion in each corner. Then they skipped to each pillow, pretended to sew it, then hopped around with a pillow each, singing:

'We're the stitching queens
dressed in sateen,
we're full of beans,
see us preen,
as we steal . . . the . . . scene!'

Sneering Simone looked surprised. Tee hee, thought Horrid Henry gleefully. If everyone's talents were as awful as that, he was a shoe-in for *Talent Tigers*.

'Lovely,' said Mrs Oddbod. 'Just lovely. And now we have William, who will play the flute.'

Weepy William put his mouth to the flute and blew. There was no sound. William stopped and stared at his flute. The mouth hole appeared to have vanished.

Everyone was looking at him. What could he do?

'Toot toot toot,' trilled William, pretending to blow. 'Toot toot toot-waaaaaah!' wailed William, bursting into tears and running off stage.

'Never mind,' said Mrs Oddbod, 'anyone could put the mouthpiece on upside down. And now we have . . .' Mrs Oddbod glanced at her paper, 'a caveman Ugga Ugg dance.'

Stone-Age Steven and Beefy Bert stomped on

stage wearing leopard-skin costumes and carrying clubs.

'UGGG!' grunted Stone-Age Steven. 'UGGG UGGG UGGG UGGG UGGG! Me cave man!'

STOMP CLUMPA CLUMP

STOMP CLUMPA CLUMP

stomped Stone-Age Steven.

STOMP CLUMPA CLUMP

STOMP CLUMPA CLUMP

stomped Beefy Bert.

'UGGA BUG UGGA BUG UGG UGG UGG,' bellowed Steven, whacking the floor with his club.

'Bert!' hissed Miss Battle-Axe. 'This isn't your talent! What are you doing on stage?'

'I dunno,' said Beefy Bert.

'Boo! Boooooo!' jeered Horrid Henry from backstage as the Cavemen thudded off.

Then Moody Margaret and Sour Susan performed their rap:

'Mar-garet, ooh ooh oooh

Mar-garet, it's all true

Mar-garet, best of the best

Pick Margaret, and dump the rest.'

Rats, thought Horrid Henry, glaring. My rap was so much better. What a waste. And why was the audience applauding?

'Booooo!' yelled Horrid Henry. 'Booooooo!'

'Another sound out of you and you will not be performing,' snapped Miss Battle-Axe.

'And now Soraya will be singing "You broke my heart in 39 pieces", accompanied by her mother on the piano,' said Mrs Oddbod hastily.

'Sing out, Soraya!' hissed her mother, pounding the piano and singing along.

'I'm singing as loud as I can,' yelled Soraya.

BANG! BANG! BANG! BANG! BANG! BANG!

went the piano.

Then Jolly Josh began to saw 'Twinkle twinkle little star' on his double bass.

Sneering Simone held her ears.

'We're next,' said Horrid Henry, grabbing hold of his billboard and whipping off the cloth.

Perfect Peter stared at the billboard.

It read:

> Il Stupendioso, world's greatest magician
> played by Henry
> Magic by Henry
> Costumes by Henry
> Props by Henry
> Sound by Henry
> Written by Henry
> Directed by Henry

'But Henry,' said Peter, 'where's my name?'

'Right here,'' said Horrid Henry, pointing.

On the back, in tiny letters, was written:

Assistant: Peter

'But no one will see that,' said Peter.

Henry snorted.

'If I put your name on the *front* of the billboard, everyone would guess the trick,' said Henry.

'No they wouldn't,' said Peter.

Honestly, thought Horrid Henry, did any magician ever have such a dreadful helper?

'I'm the star,' said Henry. 'You're lucky you're even in my show. Now shut up and get in the coffin.'

Perfect Peter was furious. That was just like Henry, to be so mean.

'Get in!' ordered Henry.

Peter put on his skeleton mask and climbed into the coffin. He was fuming.

Henry had said he'd put his name on the billboard, and then he'd written it on the back. No one would know he was the assistant. No one.

The lights dimmed. Spooky music began to play.

'Oooooooohhhh,' moaned the ghostly sounds as Horrid Henry, wearing his special long black robes studded with stars and a special magician's hat, dragged his coffin through the curtains onto the stage.

'I am Il Stupendioso, the great and powerful magician!' intoned Henry. 'Now, Il Stupendioso will perform the greatest trick ever seen. Be prepared to marvel. Be prepared to be amazed. Be prepared not to believe your eyes. I, Il Stupendioso, will wake the dead!!'

'Ooohh,' gasped the audience.

Horrid Henry swept back and forth across the stage, waving his wand and mumbling.

'First I will say the secret words of magic. Beware! Beware! Do not try this at home. Do not try this in a graveyard. Do not—' Henry's voice sank to a whisper – 'do not try this unless you're prepared for the dead . . . to walk!' Horrid Henry ended his sentence with a blood-curdling scream. The audience gasped.

Horrid Henry stood above the coffin and chanted:

'Abracadabra,
flummery flax,
voodoo hoodoo mumbo crax.
Rise and shine, corpse of mine!'

Then Horrid Henry whacked the coffin once with his wand.

Slowly Perfect Peter poked a skeleton hand out of the coffin, then withdrew it.

'Ohhhh,' went the audience. Toddler Tom began to wail.

Horrid Henry repeated the spell.

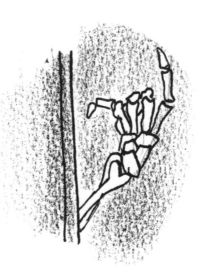

'Abracadabra, flummery flax,
voodoo hoodoo mumbo crax.
Rise and shine, bony swine!'

Then Horrid Henry whacked the coffin twice
with his wand.

This time Perfect Peter slowly raised the plastic
skull with a few tufts
of blond hair glued
to it, then lowered it
back down.

Toddler Tom
began to howl.

'And now, for the
third and final time,
I will say the magic
spell, and before your eyes, the body will rise. Stand
back . . .

'Abracadabra,
flummery flax,
voodoo hoodoo mumbo crax.
Rise and shine, here is the sign!'

And Horrid Henry whacked the coffin three times
with his wand.

The audience held its breath.

And held it.

And held it.

And held it.

'He's been dead a long time, maybe his hearing isn't so good,' said Horrid Henry. 'Rise and shine, here is the sign,' shouted Henry, whacking the coffin furiously.

Again, nothing happened.

'Rise and shine, brother of mine,' hissed Henry, kicking the coffin, 'or you'll be sorry you were born.'

I'm on strike, thought Perfect Peter. How dare Henry stick his name on the back of the billboard. And after all Peter's hard work!

Horrid Henry looked at the audience. The audience looked expectantly at Horrid Henry.

What could he do? Open the coffin and yank the body out? Yell, 'Ta da!' and run off stage? Do his famous elephant dance?

Horrid Henry took a deep breath.

'Now that's what I call *dead*,' said Horrid Henry.

'This was a difficult decision,' said Sneering Simone. Henry held his breath. He'd kill Peter later. Peter had finally risen from the coffin *after* Henry left the stage, then instead of slinking off, he'd actually said, 'Hello everyone! I'm alive!' and waved. Grrr. Well, Peter wouldn't have to pretend to be a corpse once Henry had finished with him.

'. . . a very difficult decision. But I've decided that the winner is . . .' Please not Margaret, please not Margaret, prayed Henry. Sneering Simone consulted her notes, 'The winner is the Il Stupendioso–'

'YES!!' screamed Horrid Henry, leaping to his feet. He'd done it! Fame at last! Henry Superstar was born! Yes yes yes!

Sneering Simone glared. 'As I was saying, the Il Stupendioso corpse. Great comic timing. Can someone tell me his name?'

Horrid Henry stopped dancing.

Huh?

What?

The *corpse*?

'Is that me?' said Peter. 'I won?'

'NOOOOOOOOO!' shrieked Horrid Henry.

HH'S TALENT SHOW RAP

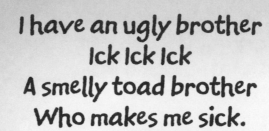

I have an ugly brother
Ick Ick Ick
A smelly toad brother
Who makes me sick.

My name is Henry
I hate fresh air
I love to laze around
On the comfy black chair

Boo to Miss Battle-Axe
World's biggest shrew
Boo to Maggie Moo-Moo
Boo to Peter too

My evil enemies try their best
Ha! I'm far too clever
Henry always wins the fight
Purple Hand rules forever

MOODY MARGARET'S
Sleepover

'**W**hat are you doing here?' said Moody Margaret, glaring.

'I'm here for the sleepover,' said Sour Susan, glaring back.

'You were uninvited, remember?' said Margaret.

'And then you invited me again, remember?' snapped Susan.

'Did not.'

'Did too. You told me last week I could come.'

'Didn't.'

'Did. You're such a meanie, Margaret,' scowled Susan. Aaaarrggghh. Why was she friends with such a moody old grouch?

Moody Margaret heaved a heavy sigh. Why was she friends with such a sour old slop bucket?

'Well, since you're here, I guess you'd better come in,' said Margaret. 'But don't expect any dessert 'cause there won't be enough for you and my *real* guests.'

Sour Susan stomped inside Margaret's house. Grrrr. She wouldn't be inviting Margaret to her next sleepover party, that's for sure.

Horrid Henry couldn't sleep. He was hot. He was hungry.

'Biscuits!' moaned his tummy. 'Give me biscuits!'

Because Mum and Dad were the meanest, most horrible parents in the world, they'd forgotten to buy more biscuits and there wasn't a single solitary crumb in the house. Henry knew because he'd searched everywhere.

'Give me biscuits!' growled his tummy. 'What are you waiting for?'

I'm going to die of hunger up here, thought Horrid Henry. And it will be all Mum and Dad's fault. They'll come in tomorrow

morning and find just a few wisps of hair and some teeth. Then they'd be sorry. Then they'd wail and gnash. But it would be too late.

'How could we have forgotten to buy chocolate biscuits?' Dad would sob.

'We deserve to be locked up forever!' Mum would shriek.

'And now there's nothing left of Henry but a tooth, and it's all our fault!' they'd howl.

Humph. Serve them right.

Wait. What an idiot he was. Why should he risk death from starvation when he knew where there was a rich stash of all sorts of yummy biscuits waiting just for him?

Moody Margaret's Secret Club tent was sure to be full to bursting with goodies! Horrid Henry hadn't raided it in ages. And so long as he was quick, no one would ever know he'd left the house.

'Go on, Henry,' urged his tummy. 'FEED ME!'

Horrid Henry didn't need to be urged twice.

Slowly, quietly, he sneaked out of bed, crept down the stairs, and tiptoed out of the back door. Then quick over the wall, and hey presto, he was in the Secret Club tent. There was Margaret's Secret Club biscuit tin, in her pathetic hiding place under a blanket. Ha!

Horrid Henry prised open the lid. Oh wow. It was filled to the brim with Chocolate Fudge Chewies! And those scrumptious Triple Chocolate Chip Marshmallow Squidgies! Henry scooped up a huge handful and stuffed them in his mouth.

Chomp. Chomp. Chomp.

Oh wow. Oh wow. Was there anything more

delicious in the whole wide world than a mouthful of nicked biscuits?

'More! More! More!' yelped his tummy.

Who was Horrid Henry to say no?

Henry reached in to snatch another mega handful . . .

BANG! SLAM! BANG!

STOMP! STOMP! STOMP!

'That's too bad, Gurinder,' snapped Margaret's voice. 'It's my party so I decide. Hurry up, Susan.'

'I am hurrying,' said Susan's voice.

The footsteps were heading straight for the Secret Club tent.

Yikes. What was Margaret doing outside at this time of night? There wasn't a moment to lose.

Horrid Henry looked around wildly. Where could he hide? There was a wicker chest at the back, where Margaret kept her dressing-up clothes. Horrid Henry leapt inside and pulled the lid shut. Hopefully, the girls wouldn't be long and he could escape home before Mum and Dad discovered he'd been out.

Moody Margaret bustled into the tent, followed by her mother, Gorgeous Gurinder, Kung-Fu Kate, Lazy

Linda, Vain Violet, Singing Soraya and Sour Susan.

'Now, girls, it's late, I want you to go straight to bed, lights out, no talking,' said Margaret's mother. 'My little Maggie Moo Moo needs her beauty sleep.'

Ha, thought Horrid Henry. Margaret could sleep for a thousand years and she'd still look like a frog.

'Yes, Mum,' said Margaret.

'Good night, girls,' trilled Margaret's mum. 'See you in the morning.'

Phew, thought Horrid Henry, lying as still as he could. He'd be back home in no time, mission safely accomplished.

'We're sleeping out here?' said Singing Soraya. 'In a tent?'

'I said it was a Secret Club sleepover,' said Margaret.

Horrid Henry's heart sank. Huh? They were planning to sleep here? Rats rats rats double rats. He was going to have to hide inside this hot dusty chest until they were asleep.

Maybe they'd all fall asleep soon, thought Horrid Henry hopefully.

Because he had to get home before Mum and Dad discovered he was missing. If they realised he'd sneaked outside, he'd be in so much trouble his life wouldn't be worth living and he might as well abandon all hope of ever watching TV or eating another biscuit until he was an old, shrivelled bag of bones struggling to chew with his one tooth and watch telly with his magnifying glass and hearing aid. Yikes!

Horrid Henry looked grimly at the biscuits clutched in his fist. Thank goodness he'd brought provisions. He might be trapped here for a very long time.

'Where's your sleeping bag, Violet?' said Margaret.

'I didn't bring one,' said Vain Violet. 'I don't like sleeping on the floor.'

'Tough,' said Margaret, 'that's where we're sleeping.'

'But I need to sleep in a bed,' whined Vain Violet. 'I don't want to sleep out here.'

'Well we do,' said Margaret.

'Yeah,' said Susan.

'I can sleep anywhere,' said Lazy Linda, yawning.

'I'm calling my mum,' said Violet. 'I want to go home.'

'Go ahead,' said Margaret. 'We don't need you, do we?'

Silence.

'Oh go on, Violet, stay,' said Gurinder.

'Yeah, stay,' said Kung-Fu Kate.

'No!' said Violet, flouncing out of the tent.

'Hummph,' said Moody Margaret. 'She's no fun anyway. Now, everyone put your sleeping bags down where I say. I need to sleep by the entrance, because I need fresh air.'

'I want to sleep by the entrance,' said Soraya.

'No,' said Margaret, 'it's my party so I decide. Susan, you go at the back because you snore.'

'Do not,' said Susan.

'Do too,' said Margaret.

'Liar.'

'Liar.'

SLAP!

SLAP!

'That's it!' wailed Susan. 'I'm calling my mum.'

'Go ahead,' said Margaret, 'see if I care, snore-box.
That'll be loads more Chocolate Fudge Chewies for
the rest of us.'

Sour Susan stood still. She'd been looking forward
to Margaret's sleepover for ages. And she still hadn't
had any of the midnight feast Margaret had promised.

'All right, I'll stay,' said Susan sourly, putting her
sleeping bag down at the back of the tent by the
dressing-up chest.

'I want to be next to Gurinder,' said Lazy Linda,
scratching her head.

'Do you have nits?' said Gurinder.

'No!' said Linda.

'You do too,' said Gurinder.

'Do not,' said Linda.

'Do too,' said Gurinder. 'I'm not sleeping next to someone who has nits.'

'Me neither,' said Kate.

'Me neither,' said Soraya.

'Don't look at me,' said Margaret. 'I'm not sleeping next to you.'

'I don't have nits!' wailed Linda.

'Go next to Susan,' said Margaret.

'But she snores,' protested Linda.

'But she has nits,' protested Susan.

'Do not.'

'Do not.'

'Nitty!'

'Snory!'

Suddenly something scuttled across the floor.

'EEEEK!' squealed Soraya. 'It's a mouse!' She scrambled onto the dressing-up chest. The lid sagged.

'It won't hurt you,' said Margaret.

'Yeah,' said Susan.

'Eeeek!' squealed Linda, shrinking back.

The lid sagged even more.

Cree—eaaak went the chest.

Aaarrrrggghhh, thought Horrid Henry, trying to squash himself down before he was squished.

'Eeeek!' squealed Gurinder, scrambling onto the chest.

CREE—EAAAAAK! went the chest.

Errrrgh, thought Horrid Henry, pushing up against the sagging lid as hard as he could.

'I can't sleep if there's a . . . mouse,' said Gurinder. She looked around nervously. 'What if it runs on top of my sleeping bag?'

Margaret sighed. 'It's only a mouse,' she said.

'I'm scared of mice,' whimpered Gurinder. 'I'm leaving!' And she ran out of the tent, wailing.

'More food for the rest of us,' said Margaret, shrugging. 'I say we feast now.'

'About time,' said Soraya.

'Let's start with the Chocolate Fudge Chewies,' said Margaret, opening the Secret Club biscuit tin. 'Everyone can have two, except for me, I get four 'cause it's my . . .'

Margaret peered into the tin. There were only a few crumbs inside.

'Who stole the biscuits?' said Margaret.

'Wasn't me,' said Susan.

'Wasn't me,' said Soraya.

'Wasn't me,' said Kate.

'Wasn't me,' said Linda.

Tee hee, thought Horrid Henry.

'One of you did, so no one is getting anything to eat until you admit it,' snapped Margaret.

'Meanie,' muttered Susan sourly.

'What did you say?' said Moody Margaret.

'Nothing,' said Susan.

'Then we'll just have to wait for the culprit to come forward,' said Margaret, scowling. 'Meanwhile, get in your sleeping bags. We're going to tell scary stories in the dark. Who knows a good one?'

'I do,' said Susan.

'Not the story about the ghost kitty-cat which drank up all the milk in your kitchen, is it?' said Margaret.

Susan scowled.

'Well, it's a true scary story,' said Susan.

'I know a real scary story,' said Kung-Fu Kate. 'It's about this monster—'

'Mine's better,' said Margaret. 'It's about a flesh-eating zombie which creeps around at night and rips off—'

'NOOOO,' wailed Linda. 'I hate being scared. I'm calling my mum to come and get me.'

'No scaredy-cats allowed in the Secret Club,' said Margaret.

'I don't care,' said Linda, flouncing out.

'It's not a sleepover unless we tell ghost stories,' said Moody Margaret. 'Turn off your torches. It won't be scary unless we're all sitting in the dark.'

Sniffle. Sniffle. Sniffle.

'I want to go home,' snivelled Soraya. 'I've never slept away from home before . . . I want my mummy.'

'What a baby,' said Moody Margaret.

Horrid Henry was cramped and hot and uncomfortable. Pins and needles were shooting up his arm. He shifted his shoulder, brushing against the lid.

There was a muffled creak.

Henry froze. Whoops. Henry prayed they hadn't heard anything.

'. . . and the zombie crept inside the tent gnashing its bloody teeth and sniffing the air for human flesh, hungry for more—'

Ow. His poor aching arm. Henry shifted position again.

Creak . . .

'What was that?' whispered Susan.

'What was what?' said Margaret.

'There was a . . . a . . . creak . . .' said Susan.

'The wind,' said Margaret. 'Anyway, the zombie sneaked into the tent and—'

'You don't think . . .' hissed Kate.

'Think what?' said Margaret.

'That the zombie . . . the zombie . . .'

I'm starving, thought Horrid Henry. I'll just eat a few biscuits really, really, really quietly—

Crunch. Crunch.

'What was that?' whispered Susan.

'What was what?' said Margaret. 'You're ruining the story.'

'That . . . crunching sound,' hissed Susan.

Horrid Henry gasped. What an idiot he was! Why hadn't he thought of this before?

Crunch. Crunch. Crunch.

'Like someone . . . someone . . . crunching on . . . bones,' whispered Kung-Fu Kate.

'Someone . . . here . . .' whispered Susan.

Tap. Horrid Henry rapped on the underside of the lid.

Tap! Tap! Tap!

'I didn't hear anything,' said Margaret loudly.

93

'It's the zombie!' screamed Susan.

'He's in here!' screamed Kate.

'AAAAARRRRRRRGHHHHHHH!'

'I'm going home!' screamed Susan and Kate. 'MUMMMMMMMMYYYY!' they wailed, running off.

Ha ha, thought Horrid Henry. His brilliant plan had worked!!! Tee hee. He'd hop out, steal the rest of the feast and scoot home. Hopefully Mum and Dad—

YANK!

Suddenly the chest lid was flung open and a torch shone in his eyes. Moody Margaret's hideous face glared down at him.

'Gotcha!' said Moody Margaret. 'Oh boy, are you in trouble. Just wait till I tell on you. Ha ha, Henry, you're dead.'

Horrid Henry climbed out of the chest and brushed a few crumbs onto the carpet.

'Just wait till I tell everyone at school about your sleepover,' said Horrid Henry. 'How you were so mean and bossy everyone ran away.'

'Your parents will punish you forever,' said Moody Margaret.

'Your name will be mud forever,' said Horrid Henry. 'Everyone will laugh at you and serves you right, Maggie Moo Moo.'

'Don't call me that,' said Margaret, glaring.

'Call you what, Moo Moo?'

'All right,' said Margaret slowly. 'I won't tell on you if you give me two packs of Chocolate Fudge Chewies.'

'No way,' said Henry. 'I won't tell on you if you give me three packs of Chocolate Fudge Chewies.'

'Fine,' said Margaret. 'Your parents are still up, I'll tell them where you are right now. I wouldn't want them to worry.'

'Go ahead,' said Henry. 'I can't wait until school tomorrow.'

Margaret scowled.

'Just this once,' said Horrid Henry. 'I won't tell on you if you won't tell on me.'

'Just this once,' said Moody Margaret. 'But never again.'

They glared at each other.

When he was king, thought Horrid Henry, anyone named Margaret would be catapulted over the walls into an oozy swamp. Meanwhile . . . on guard, Margaret. On guard. I will be avenged!

MARGARET'S SLEEPOVER RULES

1. I am the boss.
2. It's my sleepover so
I decide everything.
3. Guests must bring presents.
4. I get the most biscuits because
it's my house.
5. No boys allowed.
6. I decide where everyone sleeps.
7. No scaredy-cats allowed.
8. All guests must do what
I tell them.

If everyone follows these rules
we will have the best sleepover party
ever. If anyone disobeys they will be
sent straight home.

HORRiD HENRY'S
Autobiography

Bang! Crash! Kaboom!

Rude Ralph bounced on a chair and did his Tarzan impression.

Moody Margaret yanked Lazy Linda's hair. Linda screamed.

Stone-Age Steven stomped round the room grunting 'Ugg.'

**'Rat about town
don't need a gown.
where I'm goin'
Only fangs'll be showin,'**

shrieked Horrid Henry.

'Quiet!' barked Miss Battle-Axe. 'Settle down immediately.'

Ralph bounced.

Steven stomped.

Linda screamed.

Henry shrieked. He was the Killer Boy Rats new lead singer, blasting his music into the roaring crowd, hurling—

'HENRY, BE QUIET!' bellowed Miss Battle-Axe. 'Or playtime is cancelled. For everyone.'

Horrid Henry scowled. Why oh why did he have to come to school? Why didn't the Killer Boy Rats start a school, where you'd do nothing but scream and stomp all day? Now that's the sort of school everyone would want to go to. But no. He had to come here. When he was king all schools would just teach jousting and spying and Terminator Gladiator would be head.

Henry looked at the clock. How could it be only 9.42? It felt like he'd been sitting here for ages. What he'd give to be lounging right now on the comfy black chair, eating crisps and watching *Hog House* . . .

'Today we have a very exciting project,' said Miss Battle-Axe.

Henry groaned. Miss Battle-Axe's idea of an exciting project and his were never the same. An exciting project would be building a time machine, or a let's see who can give Henry the most chocolate competition, or counting how many times he could hit Miss Battle-Axe with a water balloon.

'We'll be writing autobiographies,' said Miss Battle-Axe.

Ha. He knew it would be something boring. Horrid Henry hated writing. All that pushing a pen across a piece of paper. Writing always made his hand ache. Writing was hard, heavy work. Why did Miss Battle-Axe try to torture him every day? Didn't she have anything better to do? Henry groaned again.

'An autobiography means the story of your life,' continued Miss Battle-Axe, glaring at him with her evil red eyes. 'Everyone will write a page about themselves and all the interesting things they've done.'

Yawn. Could his life get any worse?

Write a page? A whole entire page? What could be more boring than writing on and on about himself—

Wait a minute.

He got to write . . . about himself? The world's most fascinating boy? He could write for hours about himself! Days. Weeks. Years. Hold on . . . what was batty old Miss Battle-Axe saying now?

'. . . the really exciting part is that our autobiographies will be published in the local newspaper next week.'

Oh wow! Oh wow! Oh wow! His autobiography would be published!

This was his chance to tell the world all about being Lord High Excellent Majesty of the Purple Hand Gang. How he'd vanquished so many evil enemies. All the brilliant tricks he'd played on Peter. He'd write about the Mega-Mean Time Machine. And the Fangmangler. And the millions of times he'd defeated the Secret Club and squished Moody Margaret to a pulp! And oh yes, he'd be sure to include the time he'd turned his one line in the school play into a starring part and scored the winning goal in the class football match. But one page would barely cover one day in his life. He needed hundreds of pages . . . no, thousands of pages to write about just some of his top triumphs.

Where to begin?

'Let's start with you, Clare,' burbled Miss Battle-Axe.

'What would you put in your autobiography?'

Clare beamed. 'I walked when I was four months old, learned to read when I was two, did long division when I was three, built my first telescope when I was four, composed a symphony—'

'Thank you, Clare, I'm sure everyone will look forward to learning more about you,' said Miss Battle-Axe. 'Steven. What will—'

'Can't we just get started?' shouted Henry. 'I've got masses to write.'

'As I was saying, before I was so RUDELY interrupted,' said Miss Battle-Axe, glaring, 'Steven, what will you be writing about in your autobiography?'

'Being a caveman,' grunted Stone-Age Steven.

'Uggg.'

'Fascinating,' said Miss Battle-Axe. 'Bert! What's interesting about your life?'

'I dunno,' said Beefy Bert.

'DUNNO.'

'Right, then, everyone get to work,' said Miss Battle-Axe, fixing Horrid Henry with her basilisk stare.

Horrid Henry wrote until his hand ached. But he'd barely got to the time he tricked Margaret into eating glop before Miss Battle-Axe ordered everyone to stop.

'But I haven't finished!' shouted Horrid Henry.

'Tough,' said Miss Battle-Axe. 'Now, before we send these autobiographies to the newspaper, I'd like a few of you to read yours aloud to the class. William, let's start with you.'

Weepy William burst into tears. 'I don't want to go first,' he wailed, dabbing his eyes with some loo paper.

'Read,' said Miss Battle-Axe.

WILLIAM'S AUTOBIOGRAPHY

I was born. I cried. A few years later my brother Neil was born. I cried.
In school Toby broke my pencil. Margaret picked me last. When we had to build the Parthenon Henry took all my paper and then when I got some more it was dirty. I had to play a blade of grass in the Nativity play. I cried.
I lost every race on Sports Day. I cried. Then I got nits. On the school trip to the Ice Cream Factory I did a wee in my pants. I cried. Nothing else has ever happened to me.

'Who's next?' asked Miss Battle-Axe.

Horrid Henry's hand shot up. Miss Battle-Axe looked as if a zombie had just walked across her grave. Horrid Henry never put his hand up.

'Linda,' said Miss Battle-Axe.

Lazy Linda woke up and yawned.

LINDA'S AUTOBIOGRAPHY

I've had many nice beds in my life. First was my Moses basket. Then my cot. Then my little bed. Then my great big sleigh bed. Then my princess bed with the curtains and the yellow headboard. I've also had a lot of duvets. First my duvet had ducks on it. Then I got a new soft one with big fluffy clouds. Oooh, I am sleepy just thinking about it . . .

'We have time to hear one more,' said Miss Battle-Axe, scanning the class. Horrid Henry thought his arm would detach itself from his shoulder if

he shoved it any higher.
'Margaret,' said Miss Battle-
Axe.

Henry scowled. It was so
unfair. No one wanted to
know about that moody old
grouch.

Moody Margaret
swaggered to the front and
noisily cleared her throat.

MARGARET'S
AUTOBIOGRAPHY

Greetings, world. I'm very sad
when I think that many of you
reading this will never get to
meet someone as amazing
as me. But at least you can
read something I've written,
and you newspaper people
should save this piece of
paper, because I, Margaret,
have touched it with my very
own hands, and it's sure to be
valuable in the future when
I'm famous.

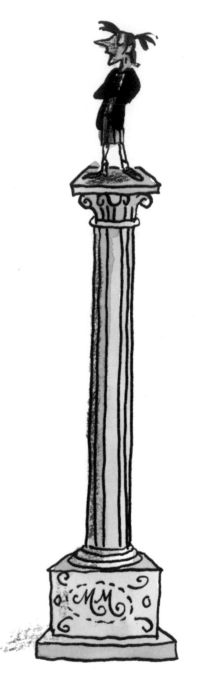

Let me tell you a few things about marvellous me. First, I am the leader of the Secret Club, which is always victorious against the pathetic and puny Purple Hand Gang next door. One reason we always destroy them, apart from my brilliant plotting, is because the Purple Hand's so-called leader, Henry, is really stupid and useless and pathetic.

Horrid Henry could not believe his ears.
'Liar!' shouted Henry. 'I always win!'
'Shh!' said Miss Battle-Axe.

Naturally, I am the best footballer the school has ever had or will ever have, and naturally I'm Captain of the Football Team. Everyone always wants to play on my team, but of course I don't let no-hopers like Henry on it. I'm also a fantastic trumpet player, and a top spy. My best toy is my Dungeon Drink Kit, which I've used many times to play great tricks on the Purple Hand Gang, which they always fall for.

But I know I'll be very famous so I'm saving my best stories for my future best-selling autobiography. I expect there will be many statues built to me all over town, and that this school will be renamed the Margaret School.

I know it's hard realising that you can never be as great as me, but get used to it!!!

Moody Margaret stopped reading and swaggered to her seat.

'Yay!' yelled Sour Susan.

'Boo!' yelled Horrid Henry.

'Boo!' yelled Rude Ralph.

'There's no booing in this class,' said Miss Battle-Axe.

Horrid Henry was outraged. Margaret's lies about him . . . published? The Purple Hand Gang always won. But the whole world would believe her lies once they read them in a newspaper. He had to stop that foul fiend. He had to show everyone what a pants-face liar Margaret really was.

But how? How? He could just try to steal her autobiography. But someone might notice it had gone missing. Or he could . . . he could . . .

The playtime bell rang. Miss Battle-Axe started collecting up all the autobiographies. Henry watched helplessly as Margaret's

pack of boasting lies went into the folder.

And then Horrid Henry knew what he had to
do. It was dangerous. It was risky. But a pirate gang
leader had to take his chances, come what may.

Horrid Henry put up his hand. 'Please, miss,
I haven't finished my autobiography yet. Could I
stay in at playtime to finish?'

Miss Battle-Axe looked at Henry as if he had just
grown an extra head. Henry . . . asking to spend
more time on work? Horrid Henry asking to skip
playtime?

'You can have five more minutes,' said Miss
Battle-Axe, mopping her brow.

Horrid Henry wrote and wrote and wrote.
When would Miss Battle-Axe leave him alone for a
moment? But there she was, stapling up drawings of
light bulbs.

'Put it in the folder with the others,' said Miss
Battle-Axe, facing the wall. Horrid Henry didn't wait
to be asked twice and grabbed the folder.

There wasn't a moment to lose. Henry rifled
through the autobiographies, removed Margaret's,
and substituted his new, improved version.

Moody Margaret peered round the door. Tee hee,
thought Horrid Henry, pushing past her. Wouldn't
she get a shock when she got her newspaper! What
he'd give to see her face.

THWACK!

The local paper dropped through the door. Henry snatched it. There was the headline:

LOCAL CHILDREN SHINE IN
FASCINATING TALES OF THEIR LIVES

Feverishly, he turned to read the class autobiographies.

MARGARET'S AUTOBIOGRAPHY

Oh woe is me, to be such a silly moody grouchy grump. I've always looked like a frog, in fact my mum took one look at me when I was born, threw me in the bin and ran screaming from the

room. I don't blame her; I scream too whenever I see my ugly warty face in the mirror. Everyone calls me Maggie Moo Moo, or Maggie Poo Poo, because I still wear nappies.

I started a Secret Club, which no one wants to join, because I am so mean and bossy. I can't even have a sleepover without everyone running away. I keep trying to beat Henry's Purple Hand Gang, but he's much too clever for me and always foils my evil plans. I live next door to Henry, but of course I don't deserve such a great honour. I really should just live in a smelly hole somewhere with all the other frogs. So, just remember, everyone, beware of being a moody, grouchy grump, or you might end up as horrible as me.

Yes! What a triumph! He was brilliant. He was a genius. What an amazing trick to write the truth about Margaret and swap it for her pack of lies.

Horrid Henry beamed. Now to enjoy his own autobiography. It was far too short, but there was always next time.

HENRY'S AUTOBIOGRAPHY

I'm a total copycat. Luckily, I live next door to the amazing Margaret, who I look up to and admire and worship more than anyone in the world. Margaret is my heroine, but I will never be as clever or as brilliant as she is, because I'm a pathetic, useless toad. I copied her amazing Secret Club, but the Purple Hand always loses. I tried to do Makeovers, but of course I couldn't. Even my own brother wants to work for her as a spy. But then, she is an empress and I'm a worm.

The most exciting thing that ever happened to me was when Margaret moved in next door. I hope that one day she will let me be the guard of the Secret Club, but I will have to work very hard to deserve it. That would be the best thing that has ever happened in my boring life.

Huh? What? That fiend! That foul fiend!

The doorbell rang.

There was Margaret, waving the newspaper. Her face was purple.

'How dare you!' she shrieked.

'How dare you!' Henry shrieked.

'I'll get you for this, Henry,' hissed Margaret.
'Just you wait, Margaret,' hissed Henry.

THE TRUE AUTOBIOGRAPHY OF HENRY

Lord High Excellent Majesty of the Purple Hand Gang, leader and boss of the secret fort and the destroyer of the Secret Club and Nappy Noodle Brothers. Wizard, star actor, footballer, trickster, genius, the scourge of evil enemies and the bulldozer of babysitters and battle-axes and demon dinner ladies and horrible cousins.

I was born in February – oh let's skip that boring bit – to the King and Queen, but sadly I was stolen by an evil wizard and dumped with…THEM. Obviously I am waiting for my real parents to collect me and take me back to the palace, but until then I am stuck with the world's most boring, mean and horrible parents in the history of the world.

To say nothing of
their son, the worm,
my so-called younger brother,
Peter. As if someone as amazing
as me could have such a nappy
noodle poopy pants for a brother. That just
proves I must have been stolen by a wizard.
There is no other possible explanation.

My greatest talent, among so many, is that I
am a genius trickster. I have played so many
amazing, fantastic tricks that it's hard even for
me to remember them all. Let's start with the
day my horrible worm brother was born...

by Henry

HORRiD HENRY
and the Nudie Foodie

'Children, I have some *thrilling* news,' burbled Mrs Oddbod.

Horrid Henry groaned. His idea of thrilling news and Mrs Oddbod's idea of thrilling news were not the same. Thrilling news would be Mutant Max replacing Mrs Oddbod as head. Thrilling news would be Miss Battle-Axe being whisked off to ancient Rome to be a gladiator. Thrilling news would be Moody Margaret dumped in a swamp  and Perfect Peter sent to prison.

Thrilling news wasn't new coat hooks and who was in the Good as Gold book.

But wait. What was Mrs Oddbod saying? 'Our school has been chosen to be a healthy-eating school. Our new healthy and nutritious school meals will be an example for schools everywhere.'

Horrid Henry sat up. What? *Healthy* eating? Oh no. Henry knew what grown-ups

meant by healthy food. Celery. Beetroot. Aubergine towers. Anything that tasted yucky and looked revolting was bound to be good for him. Anything that tasted yummy was bound to be bad. Henry had plenty of healthy eating at home. Was nowhere safe?

'And guess who's going to help make our school a beacon of healthy eating?' babbled Mrs Oddbod. 'Only the world-famous chef, Mr Nudie Foodie.'

Rude Ralph snorted.

'Nudie,' he jeered.

Mr Nudie Foodie? thought Horrid Henry. What kind of stupid name was that? Were there really parents out there whose surname was Foodie, who'd decided that the perfect name for their son was Nudie?

'And here he is, in person,' proclaimed Mrs Oddbod.

The children clapped as a shaggy-haired man wearing a red-checked apron and a chef's hat bounced to the front of the auditorium.

'From today your school will be *the* place for delicious, nutritious food,' he beamed. 'I'm not nude, it's my food that's nude! My delicious, yummalicious grub is just plain scrummy.'

Horrid Henry couldn't believe his ears. Just plain, delicious food? Why, that was *exactly* what Horrid Henry loved. Plain burgers. Plain pizzas just with cheese and nothing else. No sneaky flabby pieces of aubergine or grisly chunks of red pepper ruining the

topping. Plain chips slathered in ketchup. No funny
bits. No strange green stuff. Three cheers to more
burgers, more chips and more pizza!

Horrid Henry could see it now. Obviously, *he'd*
be asked to create the yummy new school menu of
plain, delicious food.

Monday: crisps, chips, ice cream, cake,
burgers
Tuesday: burgers, chips, crisps, chocolate
Wednesday: pizza, chips, crisps, ice cream
Thursday: chocolate cake
Friday: burgers, pizza, chips, crisps, cake,
ice cream

(after all, it was the end of the week, and nice to
celebrate). Oh, and fizzywizz drinks every day, and
chocolate milk. There! A lovely, healthy, plain,
nutritious and delicious menu that everyone would
love. Because, let's face it, at the moment school
dinners *were* horrid. They only served burgers
and chips once a week, thought Horrid Henry
indignantly. Well, he'd soon sort *that* out.

In fact, maybe *he* should be a famous chef when
he got older. Chef Henry, the burger wizard.
Happy Henry, hamburger hero. He would open a

chain of famous restaurants, called *Henry's! Where the eatin' can't be beaten!* Hmmm, well, he'd have time to improve the name, while collecting his millions every week from the restaurant tills as happy customers fought their way inside for the chance to chow down on one of Happy Henry's bun-tastic burgers. Kids everywhere would beg to eat there, safe in the knowledge that no vegetables would ever contaminate their food.

Ahhh! Horrid Henry sighed.

Mr Nudie Foodie was leaping up and down with excitement. 'And you're all going to help me make the delicious food that will be a joy to eat. Remember, just like the words to my hit song:

It's not rude
To be a dude
Who loves nude food.
Yee haw.'

'Well, Nudie,' said Mrs Oddbod. 'Uhh, I mean, Mr Foodie . . . '

'Just call me Mr Nudie Foodie,' said Mr Nudie Foodie. 'Now, who wants to be a nudie foodie and join me in the kitchen to make lunch today?'

'Me!' shouted Perfect Peter.

'Me!' shouted Clever Clare.

'I want to be a nudie foodie,' said Jolly Josh.

'I want to be a nudie foodie,' said Tidy Ted.

'I want to be a nudie foodie,' yelled Greedy Graham. 'I think.'

'A healthy school is a happy school,' said Mr Nudie Foodie, beaming. 'My motto is: Only bad food boos, when you choose yummy food. And at lunchtime today, all your parents will be coming to the cafeteria to sample our scrumptious, yummalicious, fabulicious and irresistible new food! Olé!'

Horrid Henry looked round the school kitchen. He'd never seen so many pots and pans and vats

and cauldrons. So this was where the
school glop was made. Well, not any
longer. Would they be making giant
whopper burgers in the huge frying
pans? Or vats and vats of chips in the
huge pots? Maybe they'd make pizzas in the gigantic
ovens!

The Nudie Foodie stood before Henry's class. 'This is
so exciting,' he said, bouncing up and down. 'Everyone
ready to make some delicious food?'

'Yes!' bellowed Henry's class.

'Right, then, let's get cooking,' said Mr Nudie
Foodie.

Horrid Henry stood in front of a chopping board
with Weepy William, Dizzy Dave and Fiery Fiona.
Fiery Fiona shoved Henry.

'Stop hogging the chopping board,' she hissed.

Horrid Henry shoved her back, knocking the
lumpy bag of ingredients onto the floor.

'Stop hogging it yourself,' he hissed back.

'Wah!' wailed Weepy William. 'Henry pushed
me.'

Wait. What was rolling all over the floor? It looked
like . . . it couldn't be . . .

'Group 1, here's how to slice a yummy green
pepper,' beamed Mr Nudie Foodie. 'And Group 2,

you're in charge of the tomatoes . . . Group 3, you
make the broccoli salad. Group 4 will look after the
mushrooms.'

Green pepper? Tomatoes? Broccoli? Mushrooms?
What was this muck?

'It's my yummy, scrummy, super, secret, vege-
tastic pasta sauce!' said Mr Nudie Foodie.

What? What a dirty rotten trick. Where were the
chips? Where were the burgers?

And then suddenly Horrid Henry understood
Mr Nudie Foodie's evil plan. He was going to sneak

vegetables onto the school menu. Not just a single vegetable, but loads and loads and loads of vegetables. Enough evil vegetables to kill someone a hundred times over. Boy impaled by killer carrot.

Girl chokes to death on deadly broccoli. Boy gags on toxic tomato. Henry could see the headlines now. They'd find him dead in the lunchroom, poisoned by vegetables, his limbs twisted in agony . . .

Well, *no way*. No way was this foul fiend going to trick Henry into eating vegetables.

Everyone chopped and stirred and mixed. The evil brew hissed and bubbled. Horrid Henry had never felt so cheated in his life.

Finally, the bell rang.

Mr Nudie Foodie stood by the exit with an enormous black bin bag.

'Before you leave I want you to open your lunch boxes and dump all your junk food in here. No need for that stuff today.'

'Huh?' said Rude Ralph.

'No!' wailed Greedy Graham.

'Yes!' said Mr Nudie Foodie. 'You'll thank me later.'

Horrid Henry gasped in horror as everyone threw their yummy snacks into the bag as they filed out of the kitchen and ran out for playtime. For once Henry was glad his mean, horrible parents never packed anything good in *his* lunchbox.

Was there no end to this evil man's plots? thought Horrid Henry, stomping past Mr Nudie Foodie into the hall. First, vegetable pasta sauce, then stealing everyone's sweets? What a waste. All those treats going straight into the bin . . .

'Rescue us Henry!' squealed the chocolate and crisps trapped inside the bin bag. 'Help!'

Horrid Henry didn't need to be asked twice. He crept down the hall and darted back into the school kitchen.

Sweets, here I come, thought Horrid Henry.

The kitchen was empty. Huge vats of vegetable sauce sat ready to be poured onto pasta. What horrors would Mr Nudie Foodie try to sneak on the menu tomorrow? And the next day? And the next? Just wait until the parents discovered the sauce was made of vegetables. They'd make the children eat this swill every day.

AAAAARRRRRGGGHHHHH.

And then suddenly Horrid Henry knew what he had to do. He looked longingly at the enormous black bin bag bulging with crisps and chocolate and yummy snacks. Horrid Henry gritted his teeth. Sometimes you had to think ahead. Sometimes you couldn't be distracted. Not even by doughnuts.

There wasn't a moment to lose. Any second a teacher or dinner lady could come in and foil him. He had to seize his chance to stop Mr Nudie Foodie once and for all.

Grabbing whatever was nearest, Horrid Henry emptied a tin of salt into the first vat of sauce. Into the second went a tin of mustard powder. Into the third went a bottle of vinegar. Into the fourth and final one . . .

Henry looked at the gurgling, bubbling, poisonous, reeking, rancid, toxic sauce. Take that, Nudie Foodie, thought Horrid Henry, reaching for a tub of lard.

'What are you doing, Henry?' rasped a deadly voice.

Henry froze.

'Just looking for my lunchbox,' he said, pretending to search behind the cooking pots.

Miss Battle-Axe snarled, flashing her yellow brick teeth. She pointed to the door. Horrid Henry ran out.

Phew. What a lucky escape. Shame he hadn't completed his mission, but three vats out of four wasn't bad.

Anyway, the fourth pot was sure to be disgusting, even without extra dollops of lard.

You are dead meat, Mr Nudie Foodie, thought Horrid Henry.

'Parents, children, prepare yourselves for a taste sensation!' said Mr Nudie Foodie, ladling out pasta and sauce.

Lazy Linda's mother took a big forkful. 'Hmm, doesn't this look yummy!' she said.

'It's about time this school served proper food,' said Moody Margaret's mum, shovelling an enormous spoonful into her mouth.

'I couldn't agree more,' said Tidy Ted's dad, scooping up pasta.

'BLECCCCHHHHH!' spluttered Margaret's mother, spitting it out all over Aerobic Al's dad.

Her face was purple. 'That's disgusting! My Maggie Moo-Moo won't be touching a drop of that!'

'What are you trying to do, poison people?!' screamed Aerobic Al's Dad. His face was green.

'I'm not eating this muck!' shouted Clever Clare's Mum. 'And Clare certainly isn't.'

'But . . . but . . .' gasped Mr Nudie Foodie. 'This sauce is my speciality, it's delicious, it's—' he took a mouthful.

'Uggghhhh,' he said, spewing it all over Mrs Oddbod. 'It *is* disgusting.'

Wow, thought Horrid Henry. Wow. Could the sauce really be *so* bad? He had to try it. Would he get the salty, the mustardy, the vinegary, or just the plain disgusting vegetably?

Henry picked up a tiny forkful of pasta, put it in his mouth and swallowed.

He was still breathing. He was still alive. Everyone at his table was slurping up the food and beaming.

Everyone at the other tables was coughing and
choking and spitting . . .

Horrid Henry took another teeny tiny taste.

The sauce was . . . delicious. It was much nicer
than the regular glop they served at lunchtime with
pasta. It was a million billion times nicer. And he had
just . . . he had just . . .

'Is this some kind of joke?' gasped Mrs Oddbod,
gagging. 'Mr Nudie Foodie, you are toast! Leave here
at once!'

Mr Nudie Foodie slunk off.

'NOOOOO!' screamed Horrid Henry. 'It's
yummy! Don't go!'

Everyone stared at Horrid Henry.
'Weird,' said Rude Ralph.

HORRiD HENRY'S FOOD PYRAMID
This is MY food pyramid. Forget vegetables –
when I'm king, this is what kids will get to eat every day.

The ice cream and fizzywizz group. One to two servings every day.

The burger and chips group. Buy from Gobble & Go if possible. Three servings a day, plus ketchup.

Sweets – the most important group! At least ten servings a day. Big Boppers. Toffees.

HORRID HENRY
and the Mad Professor

Horrid Henry grabbed the top secret sweet tin he kept hidden under his bed. It was jampacked with all his favourites: Big Boppers. Nose Pickers. Dirt Balls. Hot Snot. Gooey Chewies. Scrunchy Munchies. Yummy!!!

Hmmm boy! Horrid Henry's mouth watered as he prised off the lid. Which to have first?

A Dirt Ball?

Or a Gooey Chewy? Actually, he'd just scoff the lot. It had been ages since he'd . . .

Huh?

Where were all his chocolates? Where were all his sweets? Who'd nicked them? Had Margaret invaded his room? Had Peter sneaked in?

How dare— Oh. Horrid Henry suddenly remembered. *He'd* eaten them all.

Rats.

Rats.

Triple rats.

Well, he'd just have to go and buy more. He was sure to have loads of pocket money left.

Chocolate, here I come, thought Horrid Henry, heaving his bones and dashing over to his skeleton bank.

He shook it. Then he shook it again.

There wasn't even a rattle.

How could he have *no* money and *no* sweets? It was so unfair! Just last

night Peter had been boasting about having £7.48 in *his* piggy bank. And loads of sweets left over from Hallowe'en. Horrid Henry scowled. Why did Peter *always* have money? Why did he, Henry, *never* have money?

Money was totally wasted on Peter. What was the point of Peter having pocket money since he never spent it? Come to think of it, what was the point of Peter having sweets since he never ate them?

There was a shuffling, scuttling noise, then Perfect Peter dribbled into Henry's bedroom carrying all his soft toys.

'Get out of my room, worm!' bellowed Horrid Henry, holding his nose. 'You're stinking it up.'

'I am not,' said Peter.

'Are too, smelly pants.'

'I do not have smelly pants,' said Peter.

'Do too, woofy, poofy, pongy pants.'

Peter opened his mouth, then closed it.

'Henry, will you play with me?' said Peter.

'No.'

'Please?'

'No!'

'Pretty please?'

'No!!'

'But we could play school with all my cuddly toys,' said Peter. 'Or have a tea party with them . . .'

'For the last time, NOOOOOOO!' screamed Horrid Henry.

'You *never* play with me,' said Perfect Peter.

'That's 'cause you're a toad-faced nappy wibble bibble,' said Horrid Henry. 'Now go away and leave me alone.'

'Mum! Henry's calling me names again!' screamed Peter. 'He called me wibble bibble.'

'Henry! Don't be horrid!' shouted Mum.

'I'm not being horrid, Peter's annoying me!' yelled Henry.

'Henry's annoying *me*!' yelled Peter.

'Make him stop!' screamed Henry and Peter.

Mum ran into the room.

'Boys. If you can't play nicely then leave each other alone,' said Mum.

'Henry won't play with me,' wailed Peter. 'He *never* plays with me.'

'Henry! Why can't you play with your brother?'

said Mum. 'When I was little Ruby and I played beautifully together all the time.'

Horrid Henry scowled.

'Because he's a wormy worm,' said Henry.

'Mum! Henry just called me a wormy worm,' wailed Peter.

'Don't call your brother names,' said Mum.

'Peter only wants to play stupid baby games,' said Henry.

'I do not,' said Peter.

'If you're not going to play together then you can

do your chores,' said Mum.

'I've done mine,' said Peter. 'I fed Fluffy, cleaned out the litter tray *and* tidied my room.'

Mum beamed. 'Peter, *you* are the best boy in the world.'

Horrid Henry scowled. He'd been far too busy reading his comics to empty the wastepaper bins and tidy

his room. He stuck out his tongue at Peter behind Mum's back.

'Henry's making horrible faces at me,' said Peter.

'Henry, *please* be nice for once and play with Peter,' said Mum. She sighed and left the room.

Henry glared at Peter.

Peter glared at Henry.

Horrid Henry was about to push Peter out the door when suddenly he had a brilliant, spectacular idea. It was so brilliant and so spectacular that Horrid Henry couldn't believe he was still standing in his bedroom and hadn't blasted off into outer space trailing clouds of glory. Why had he never thought of this before? It was magnificent. It was genius. One day he would start Henry's Genius Shop, where people would pay a million pounds to buy his super fantastic ideas. But until then . . .

'Okay Peter, I'll play with you,' said Horrid Henry. He smiled sweetly.

Perfect Peter could hardly believe his ears.

'You'll . . . *play* with me?' said Perfect Peter.

'Sure,' said Horrid Henry.

'What do you want to play?' asked Peter cautiously. The last time Peter could remember Henry playing with him they'd played Cannibals and Dinner. Peter had had to be dinner . . .

'Let's play Robot and Mad Professor,' said Henry.

'Okay,' said Perfect Peter. Wow. That sounded a lot more exciting than his usual favourite game – writing lists of vegetables or having ladybird tea parties with his stuffed toys. He'd probably have to be the robot, and do what Henry said, but it would be worth it, to play such a fun game.

'I'll be the robot,' said Horrid Henry.

Peter's jaw dropped.

'Go on,' said Henry. 'You're the mad professor. Tell me what to do.'

Wow. Henry was even letting *him* be the mad professor! Maybe he'd been wrong about Henry . . . maybe Henry had been struck by lightning and changed into a nice brother . . .

'Robot,' ordered Perfect Peter. 'March around the room.'

Horrid Henry didn't budge.

'Robot!' said Peter. 'I order you to march.'

'Pro—fes—sor! I—need—twenty-five p—to—move,' said Henry in a robotic voice. 'Twenty-five p. Twenty-five p. Twenty-five p.'

'Twenty-five p?' said Peter.

'That's the rules of Robot and Mad Professor,' said Henry, shrugging.

'Okay Henry,' said Peter, rummaging in his bank. He handed Henry twenty-five p.

Yes! thought Horrid Henry.

Horrid Henry took a few stiff steps, then slowed down and stopped.

'More,' said robotic Henry. 'More. My batteries have run down. More.'

Perfect Peter handed over another twenty-five p.

Henry lurched around for a few more steps, crashed into the wall and collapsed on the floor.

'I need sweets to get up,' said the robot. 'Fetch me sweets. Systems overload. Sweets. Sweets. Sweets.'

Perfect Peter dropped two sweets into Henry's hand. Henry twitched his foot.

'More,' said the robot. 'Lots more.'

Perfect Peter dropped four more sweets. Henry jerked up into a sitting position.

'I will now tell you my top secret—secret—secret—secret—' stuttered Horrid Henry. 'Cross—my—palm—with—silver and sweets . . .' He held out his robot hands. Peter filled them.

Tee hee.

'I want to be the robot now,' said Peter.

'Okay, robot,' said Henry. 'Run upstairs and empty all the waste-paper baskets. Bet you can't do it in thirty seconds.'

'Yes I can,' said Peter.

'Nah, you're too rusty and puny,' said Horrid Henry.

'Am not,' said Peter.

'Then prove it, robot,' said Henry.

'But aren't you going to give me—' faltered Peter.

'MOVE!' bellowed Henry. 'They don't call me the MAD professor for nothing!!!'

Playing Robot and Mad Professor was a bit less fun than Peter had anticipated. Somehow, his piggy bank was now empty and Henry's skeleton bank was full. And somehow most of Peter's Hallowe'en sweets were now in Henry's sweet box.

Robot and Mad Professor was the most fun Henry had ever had playing with Peter. Now that he had all Peter's money and all Peter's sweets, could he trick Peter into doing all his chores as well?

'Let's play school,' said Peter. That would be safe. There was no way Henry could trick him playing *that* . . .

'I've got a better idea,' said Henry. 'Let's play Slaves and Masters. You're the slave. I order you to . . .'

153

'No,' interrupted Peter. 'I don't want to.' Henry couldn't make him.

'Okay,' said Henry. 'We can play school. You can be the tidy monitor.'

Oh! Peter loved being tidy monitor.

'We're going to play Clean Up The Classroom!' said Henry. 'The classroom is in here. So, get to work.'

Peter looked around the great mess of toys and dirty clothes and comics and empty wrappers scattered all over Henry's room.

'I thought we'd start by taking the register,' said Peter.

'Nah,' said Henry. 'That's the baby way to play school. You have to start by tidying the classroom. You're the tidy monitor.'

'What are you?' said Peter.

'The teacher, of course,' said Henry.

'Can I be the teacher next?' said Peter.

'Sure,' said Henry. 'We'll swap after you finish your job.'

Henry lay on his bed and read his comic and stuffed the rest of Peter's sweets into his mouth. Peter tidied.

Ah, this was the life.

'It's very quiet in here,' said Mum, popping her head round the door. 'What's going on?'

'Nothing,' said Horrid Henry.

'Why is Peter tidying your room?' said Mum.

''Cause he's the tidy monitor,' said Henry.

Perfect Peter burst into tears. 'Henry's taken all my money and all my sweets and made me do all his chores,' he wailed.

'Henry!' shouted Mum. 'You horrid boy!'

On the bad side, Mum made Henry give Peter back all his money. But on the good side, all his chores were done for the week. And he couldn't give Peter back his sweets because he'd eaten them all.

Result!

Mum is always telling me about how beautifully
she and Aunt Ruby played together.
Ha. Look at these pics I just found . . .

HORRiD HENRY'S
Horrid Weekend

'**N**OOOOOOOOO!' screamed Horrid Henry. 'I don't want to spend the weekend with Steve.'

'Don't be horrid, Henry,' said Mum. 'It's very kind of Aunt Ruby to invite us down for the weekend.'

'But I hate Aunt Ruby!' shrieked Henry. 'And I hate Steve and I hate you!'

'I can't wait to go,' said Perfect Peter.

'Shut up, Peter!' howled Henry.

'Don't tell your brother to shut up,' shouted Mum.

'Shut up! Shut up! Shut up!' And Horrid Henry fell to the floor wailing and screaming and kicking.

Stuck-Up Steve was Horrid Henry's hideous cousin. Steve hated Henry. Henry hated him. The last time Henry had seen Steve, Henry had tricked him into thinking there was a monster under his bed. Steve had sworn revenge. Then there was the other time at the restaurant when . . . well, Horrid Henry thought it would be a good idea to avoid Steve until his cousin was grown-up and in prison for crimes against humanity.

And now his mean, horrible parents were forcing him to spend a whole precious weekend with the

toadiest, wormiest, smelliest boy who ever slimed out of a swamp.

Mum sighed. 'We're going and that's that. Ruby says Steve is having a lovely friend over so that should be extra fun.'

Henry stopped screaming and kicking. Maybe Steve's friend wouldn't be a stuck-up monster. Maybe *he'd* been forced to waste his weekend with Steve, too. After all, who'd volunteer to spend time with Steve? Maybe together they could squish Stuck-Up Steve once and for all.

Ding dong.

Horrid Henry, Perfect Peter, Mum and Dad stood outside Rich Aunt Ruby's enormous house on a grey, drizzly day. Steve opened the massive front door.

'Oh,' he sneered. 'It's you.'

Steve opened the present Mum had brought. It was a small flashlight. Steve put it down.

'I already have a much better one,' he said.

'Oh,' said Mum.

Another boy stood beside him. A boy who looked vaguely familiar. A boy . . . Horrid Henry gasped. Oh no. It was Bill. Bossy Bill. The horrible son of Dad's boss. Henry had once tricked Bill into photocopying his bottom. Bill had sworn revenge. Horrid Henry's insides turned to jelly. Trust Stuck-Up Steve to be

friends with Bossy Bill. It was bad enough being trapped in a house with one Arch-Enemy. Now he was stuck in a house with TWO . . .

Stuck-up Steve scowled at Henry. 'You're wearing that old shirt of mine,' he said. 'Don't your parents ever buy you new clothes?'

Bossy Bill snorted.

'Steve,' said Aunt Ruby. 'Don't be rude.'

'I wasn't,' said Steve. 'I was just asking. No harm in asking, is there?'

'No,' said Horrid Henry. He smiled at Steve. 'So when will Aunt Ruby buy you a new face?'

'Henry,' said Mum. 'Don't be rude.'

'I was just asking,' said Henry. 'No harm in asking, is there?' he added, glaring at Steve.

Steve glared back.

Aunt Ruby beamed. 'Henry, Steve and Bill are taking you to their friend Tim's paintballing party.'

'Won't that be fun,' said Mum.

Peter looked frightened.

'Don't worry, Peter,' said Aunt Ruby, 'you can help me plant seedlings while the older boys are out.'

Peter beamed. 'Thank you,' he said. 'I don't like paintballing. Too messy and scary.'

Paintballing! Horrid Henry loved paintballing. The chance to splat Steve and Bill with ooey gooey globs of paint . . . hmmm, maybe the weekend was looking up.

'Great!' said Horrid Henry.

'How nice,' said Rich Aunt Ruby, 'you boys already know each other. Think how much fun you're all going to have sharing Steve's bedroom together.'

Uh-oh, thought Horrid Henry.

'Yeah!' said Stuck-Up Steve. 'We're looking forward to sharing a room with Henry.' His piggy eyes gleamed.

'Yeah!' said Bossy Bill. 'I can't wait.' His piggy eyes gleamed.

'Yeah,' said Horrid Henry. He wouldn't be sleeping a wink.

Horrid Henry looked around the enormous high-ceilinged bedroom he'd be sharing with his two evil enemies for two very long days and one very long night. There was a bunk-bed, which Steve and Bill had already nabbed, and two single beds. Steve's bedroom shelves were stuffed with zillions of new toys and games, as usual.

Bill and Steve smirked at each other. Henry scowled at them. What were they plotting?

'Don't you dare touch my Super-Blooper Blaster,' said Steve.

'Don't you dare touch my Demon Dagger Sabre,' said Bill.

A Super-Blooper Blaster! A Demon Dagger Sabre! Trust Bill and Steve to have the two best toys in the world . . . Rats.

'Don't worry,' said Henry. 'I don't play with baby toys.'

'Oh yeah,' said Stuck-Up Steve. 'Bet you're too much of a baby to jump off my top bunk onto your bed.'

'Am not,' said Henry.

'We're not allowed to jump on beds,' said Perfect Peter.

'We're not allowed,' mimicked Steve. 'I thought you were too poor to even *have* beds.'

'Ha ha,' said Henry.

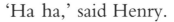

'Chicken. Chicken. Scaredy-cat,' sneered Bossy Bill.

'Squawk!' said Stuck-Up Steve. 'I knew you'd be too scared, chicken.'

That did it. *No* one called Horrid Henry chicken and lived. As if he, Henry, leader of a pirate gang, would be afraid to jump off a top bunk. Ha.

'Don't do it, Henry,' said Perfect Peter.

'Shut up, worm,' said Henry.

'But it's so high,' squealed Peter, squeezing his eyes shut.

Horrid Henry clambered up the ladder and stepped onto the top bunk. 'It's nothing,' he lied.

'I've jumped off MUCH higher.'

'Well, go on then,' said Stuck-Up Steve.

Boing! Horrid Henry bounced.

Boing! Horrid Henry bounced higher. Whee! This bed was very springy.

'We're waiting, chicken,' said Bossy Bill.

BOING! BOING! Horrid Henry bent his knees, then — leap! He jumped onto the single bed below.

SMASH!

Horrid Henry crashed to the floor as the bed collapsed beneath him.

Huh? What? How could he have broken the bed? He hadn't heard any breaking sounds.

It was as if . . . as if . . .

Mum, Dad and Aunt Ruby ran into the room.

'Henry broke the bed,' said Stuck-Up Steve.

'We tried to stop him,' said Bossy Bill, 'but Henry insisted on jumping.'

'But . . . but . . .' said Horrid Henry.

'Henry!' wailed Mum. 'You horrid boy.'

'How could you be so horrid?' said Dad. 'No pocket money for a year. Ruby, I'm so sorry.'

Aunt Ruby pursed her lips. 'These things happen,' she said.

'And no paintballing party for you,' said Mum.

What?

'No!' wailed Henry.

Then Horrid Henry saw a horrible sight. Behind Aunt Ruby's back, Steve and Bill were covering their mouths and laughing. Henry realised the terrible truth. Bill and Steve had tricked him. *They'd* broken the bed. And now *he'd* got the blame.

'But I didn't break it!' screamed Henry.

'Yes you did, Henry,' said Peter. 'I saw you.'

AAAARRRRGGGGHHHH! Horrid Henry leapt at Peter. He was a storm god hurling thunderbolts at a foolish mortal.

'AAAIIIEEEEEE!' squealed Perfect Peter.

'Henry! Stop it!' shrieked Mum. 'Leave your brother alone.'

Nah nah ne nah nah mouthed Steve behind Aunt Ruby's back.

'Isn't it lovely how nicely the boys are playing together?' said Aunt Ruby.

'Yes, isn't it?' said Mum.

'Not surprising,' said Aunt Ruby, beaming. 'After

all, Steve is such a polite, friendly boy, I've never met anyone who didn't love him.'

Snore! Snore! Snore!

Horrid Henry lay on a mattress listening to hideous snoring sounds. He'd stayed awake for hours, just in case they tried anything horrible, like pouring water on his head, or stuffing frogs in his bed. Which was what he was going to do to Peter, the moment he got home.

Henry had just spent the most horrible Saturday of his life. He'd begged to go to the paintballing party.

He'd pleaded to go to the paintballing party. He'd screamed about going to the paintballing party. But no. His mean, horrible parents wouldn't budge. And it was all Steve and Bill's fault. They'd tripped him going down the stairs.

They'd kicked him under the table at dinner (and then complained that he was kicking *them*). And every time Aunt Ruby's back was turned they stuck out their tongues and jeered: 'We're going paintballing, and you're not.'

He had to get to that party. And he had to be revenged. But how? How? His two Arch-Enemies had banded together and struck the first blow. Could he booby-trap their beds and remove a few slats? Unfortunately, everyone would know *he'd* done it and he'd be in even more trouble than he was now.

Scare them? Tell them there was a monster under the bed? Hmmm. He knew Steve was as big a scaredy-cat as Peter. But he'd already done that once. He didn't think Steve would fall for it again.

Get them into trouble? Turn them against each other? Steal their best toys and hide them? Hmmm. Hmmm. Horrid Henry thought and thought. He had to be revenged. He had to.

Tweet tweet. It was Sunday morning. The birds were singing. The sun was shining. The—

Yank!

Bossy Bill and Stuck-Up Steve pulled off his duvet.

'Nah na ne nah nah, we-ee beat you,' crowed Bill.

'Nah na ne nah nah, we got you into trouble,' crowed Steve.

Horrid Henry scowled. Time to put Operation Revenge into action.

'Bill thinks you're bossy, Steve,' said Henry. 'He told me.'

'Didn't,' said Bossy Bill.

'And Steve thinks you're stuck-up, Bill,' added Henry sweetly.

'No I don't,' said Steve.

'Then why'd you tell me that?' said Horrid Henry.

Steve stuck his nose in the air. 'Nice try Henry, you big loser,' said Stuck-Up Steve. 'Just ignore him, Bill.'

'Henry, it's not nice to tell lies,' said Perfect Peter.

'Shut up, worm,' snarled Horrid Henry.

Rats.

Time for plan B.

Except he didn't have a plan B.

'I can't wait for Tim's party,' said Bossy Bill. 'You never know what's going to happen.'

'Yeah, remember when he told us he was having a pirate party and instead we went to the Wild West Theme Park!' said Steve.

'Or when he said we were having a sleepover, and instead we all went to a Manic Buzzards concert.'

'And Tim gives the best party bags. Last year everyone got a Deluxe Demon Dagger Sabre,' said Steve. 'Wonder what he'll give this year? Oh, I forgot, Henry won't be coming to the party.'

'Too bad you can't come, Henry,' sneered Bossy Bill.

'Yeah, too bad,' sneered Stuck-Up Steve. 'Not.'

ARRRRGGGHH. Horrid Henry's blood boiled. He couldn't decide what was worse, listening to them crow about having got him into so much trouble, or brag about the great party they were going to and he wasn't.

'I can't wait to find out what surprises he'll have in store this year,' said Bill.

'Yeah,' said Steve.

Who cares? thought Horrid Henry. Unless Tim was planning to throw Bill and Steve into a shark tank. That would be a nice surprise. Unless of course . . .

And then suddenly Horrid Henry had a brilliant, spectacular idea. It was so brilliant, and so spectacular, that for a moment he wondered whether he could stop himself from flinging open the window and shouting his plan out loud. Oh wow. Oh wow. It was risky. It was dangerous. But if it worked, he would have the best revenge ever in the history of the world. No, the history of the solar system. No, the history of the universe!

It was an hour before the party. Horrid Henry was counting the seconds until he could escape.

Aunt Ruby popped her head round the door waving a note.

'Letter for you boys,' she said. Steve snatched it and tore it open.

> Dear Steve and Bill
>
> Party of the year update. Everyone must come wearing pyjamas (you'll find out why later, but don't be surprised if we all end up in a film – shhhh). It'll be a real laugh. Make sure to bring your favourite soft toys too, and wear your fluffiest slippers. Hollywood, here we come!
>
> Tim

'Wow,' said Bill.

'Wow,' said Steve.

'He must be planning something *amazing*,' said Bill.

'I bet we're all going to be acting in a film!' said Steve.

'Yeah!' said Bill.

'Too bad *you* won't, Henry,' said Stuck-Up Steve.

'You're so lucky,' said Henry. 'I wish I were going.'

Mum looked at Dad.

Dad looked at Mum.

Henry held his breath.

'Well, you can't, Henry, and that's final,' said Mum.

'It's so unfair!' shrieked Henry.

Henry's parents dropped Steve and Bill off at Tim's party on their way home. Steve was in his blue bunny pyjamas and blue bunny fluffy slippers, and clutching a panda.

Bill was in his yellow duckling pyjamas and yellow duckling fluffy slippers, and clutching his monkey.

'Shame you can't come, Henry,' said Steve, smirking. 'But we'll be sure to tell you all about it.'

'Do,' said Henry, as Mum drove off.

Horrid Henry heard squeals of laughter at Hoity-Toity Tim's front door. Bill and Steve stood frozen. Then they started to wave frantically at the car.

'Are they saying something?' said Mum, glancing in the rear-view mirror.

'Nah, just waving goodbye,' said Horrid Henry. He rolled down his window.

'Have fun, guys!'

It's obvious my horrible cousin Stuck-Up Steve
and my evilest enemy Bossy Bill are destined
for prison when they grow up.

But until that happy day here is what
Mystic Henry sees in their foul future.

HORRID HENRY and the
Abominable Snowman

oody Margaret took aim.

Thwack!

A snowball whizzed past and smacked Sour Susan in the face.

'AAAAARRGGHHH!' shrieked Susan.

'Ha ha, got you,' said Margaret.

'You big meanie,' howled Susan, scooping up a fistful of snow and hurling it at Margaret.

Thwack!

Susan's snowball smacked Moody Margaret in the face.

'OWWWW!' screamed Margaret. 'You've blinded me.'

'Good!' screamed Susan.

'I hate you!' shouted Margaret, shoving Susan.

'I hate you more!' shouted Susan, pushing Margaret.

Splat! Margaret toppled into the snow.

Splat! Susan toppled into the snow.

'I'm going home to build my own snowman,' sobbed Susan.

'Fine. I'll win without you,' said Margaret.

'Won't!'

'Will! I'm going to win, copycat,' shrieked Margaret.

'*I'm* going to win,' shrieked Susan. 'I kept my best ideas secret.'

'Win? Win what?' demanded Horrid Henry, stomping down his front steps in his snow boots and swaggering over. Henry could hear the word *win* from miles away.

'Haven't you heard about the competition?' said Sour Susan. 'The prize is—'

'Shut up! Don't tell him,' shouted Moody Margaret, packing snow onto her snowman's head.

Win? Competition? Prize? Horrid Henry's ears quivered. What secret were they trying to keep from him? Well, not for long. Horrid Henry was an expert at extracting information.

'Oh, the competition. I know all about *that*,' lied Horrid Henry. 'Hey, great snowman,' he added, strolling casually over to Margaret's snowman and pretending to admire her work.

Now, what should he do? Torture? Margaret's ponytail was always a tempting target. And snow down her jumper would make her talk.

What about blackmail? He could spread some great rumours about Margaret at school. Or . . .

'Tell me about the competition or the ice guy gets it,' said Horrid Henry suddenly, leaping over to the snowman and putting his hands round its neck.

'You wouldn't dare,' gasped Moody Margaret.

Henry's mittened hands got ready to push.

'Bye bye, head,' hissed Horrid Henry. 'Nice knowing you.'

Margaret's snowman wobbled.

'Stop!' screamed Margaret. 'I'll tell you. It doesn't

matter 'cause you'll never ever win.'

'Keep talking,' said Horrid Henry warily, watching out in case Susan tried to ambush him from behind.

'Frosty Freeze are having a best snowman competition,' said Moody Margaret, glaring. 'The winner gets a year's free supply of ice cream. The judges will decide tomorrow morning. Now get away from my snowman.'

Horrid Henry walked off in a daze, his jaw dropping. Margaret and Susan pelted him with snowballs but Henry didn't even notice. Free ice cream for a year direct from the Frosty Freeze Ice

Cream factory. Oh wow! Horrid Henry couldn't believe it. Mum and Dad were so mean and horrible they hardly ever let him have ice cream. And when they did, they never *ever* let him put on his own hot fudge sauce and whipped cream and sprinkles. Or even scoop the ice cream himself. Oh no.

Well, when he won the Best Snowman Competition they couldn't stop him gorging on Chunky Chocolate Fab Fudge Caramel Delight, or Vanilla Whip Tutti-Fruitti Toffee Treat. Oh boy! Henry could taste that glorious ice cream now. He'd live on ice cream. He'd bathe in ice cream. He'd sleep in ice cream. Everyone from school would turn up at his house when the Frosty Freeze truck arrived bringing his weekly barrels. No matter how much they begged, Horrid Henry would send them all away. No way was he sharing a drop of his precious ice cream with *anyone*.

And all he had to do was to build the best

snowman in the neighbourhood. Pah! Henry's
was sure to be the winner. He would build the
biggest snowman of all. And not just a snowman.
A snowman with claws, and horns, and fangs. A
vampire-demon-monster snowman. An Abominable
Snowman. Yes!

Henry watched Margaret and Susan rolling snow
and packing their saggy snowman. Ha. Snow heap,
more like.

'You'll never win with *that*,' jeered Horrid Henry.
'Your snowman is pathetic.'

'Better than yours,' snapped Margaret.

Horrid Henry rolled his eyes.

'Obviously, because I haven't started mine yet.'

'We've got a big head start on you, so ha ha ha,' said Susan. 'We're building a ballerina snowgirl.'

'Shut up, Susan,' screamed Margaret.

A ballerina snowgirl? What a stupid idea. If that was the best they could do Henry was sure to win.

'Mine will be the biggest, the best, the most gigantic snowman ever seen,' said Horrid Henry. 'And much better than your stupid snow dwarf.'

'Fat chance,' sneered Margaret.

'Yeah, Henry,' sneered Susan. 'Ours is the best.'

'No way,' said Horrid Henry, starting to roll a gigantic ball of snow for Abominable's big belly. There was no time to lose.

Roll. Roll. Roll.

Up the path, down the path, across the garden, down the side, back and forth, back and forth, Horrid Henry

190

rolled the biggest ball of snow ever seen.

'Henry, can I build a snowman with you?' came a little voice.

'No,' said Henry, starting to carve out some clawed feet.

'Oh please,' said Peter. 'We could build a great big one together. Like a bunny snowman, or a—'

'No!' said Henry. 'It's *my* snowman. Build your own.'

'Muuuummmm!' wailed Peter. 'Henry won't let me build a snowman with him.'

'Don't be horrid, Henry,' said Mum. 'Why don't you build one together?'

'NO!!!' said Horrid Henry. He wanted to make his *own* snowman.

If he built a snowman with his stupid worm brother, he'd have to share the prize. Well, no way. He wanted all that ice cream for himself. And his Abominable Snowman was sure to be the best. Why share a prize when you didn't have to?

'Get away from my snowman, Peter,' hissed Henry.

Perfect Peter snivelled. Then he started to roll a tiny ball of snow.

'And get your own snow,' said Henry. 'All this is mine.'

'Muuuuuum!' wailed Peter. 'Henry's hogging all the snow.'

'We're done,' trilled Moody Margaret. 'Beat *this* if you can.'

Horrid Henry looked at Margaret and Susan's snowgirl, complete with a big pink tutu wound round the waist. It was as big as Margaret.

'That old heap of snow is nothing compared to *mine*,' bragged Horrid Henry.

Moody Margaret and Sour Susan looked at Henry's Abominable Snowman, complete with Viking horned helmet, fangs, and hairy scary claws.

It was a few centimetres taller than Henry.

'Nah nah ne nah nah, mine's bigger,' boasted Henry.

'Nah nah ne nah nah, mine's better,' boasted Margaret.

'How do you like *my* snowman?' said Peter. 'Do you think *I* could win?'

Horrid Henry stared at Perfect Peter's tiny snowman. It didn't even have a head, just a long, thin, lumpy body with two stones stuck in the top for eyes.

Horrid Henry howled with laughter.

'That's the worst snowman I've ever seen,' said Henry. 'It doesn't even have a head. That's a snow carrot.'

'It is not,' wailed Peter. 'It's a big bunny.'

'Henry! Peter! Suppertime,' called Mum.

Henry stuck out his tongue at Margaret.

'And don't you dare touch my snowman.'

Margaret stuck out her tongue at Henry.

'And don't you dare touch *my* snowgirl.'

'I'll be watching you, Margaret.'

'I'll be watching *you*, Henry.'
They glared at each other.

Henry woke.

What was that noise? Was Margaret sabotaging his snowman? Was Susan stealing his snow?

Horrid Henry dashed to the window.

Phew. There was his Abominable Snowman, big as ever, dwarfing every other snowman in the street. Henry's was definitely the biggest, and the best. Umm boy, he could taste that Triple Fudge Gooey Chocolate Chip Peanut Butter Marshmallow Custard ice cream right now.

Horrid Henry climbed back into bed.

A tiny doubt nagged him.

Was his snowman *definitely* bigger than Margaret's?

'Course it was, thought Henry.

'Are you sure?' rumbled his tummy.

'Yeah,' said Henry.

'Because I really want that ice cream,' growled his tummy. 'Why don't you double-check?'

Horrid Henry got out of bed.

He was sure his was bigger and better than Margaret's. He was absolutely sure his was bigger and better.

But what if—

I can't sleep without checking, thought Henry.

Tip toe.

Tip toe.

Tip toe.

Horrid Henry slipped out of the front door.

The whole street was silent and white and frosty. Every house had a snowman in front. All of them much smaller than Henry's, he noted with satisfaction.

And there was his Abominable Snowman looming up, Viking horns scraping the sky. Horrid Henry gazed at him proudly. Next to him was Peter's pathetic pimple, with its stupid black stones. A snow lump, thought Henry.

Then he looked over at Margaret's snowgirl. Maybe it had fallen down, thought Henry hopefully. And if it hadn't maybe he could help it on its way . . .

He looked again. And again. That evil fiend!
Margaret had sneaked an extra ball of snow on
top, complete with a huge flowery hat.

That little cheater, thought Horrid Henry
indignantly. She'd sneaked out after bedtime and
made hers bigger than his. How dare she? Well, he'd
fix Margaret. He'd add more snow to his right away.
Horrid Henry looked around. Where could he

find more snow? He'd already used up every drop on his front lawn to build his giant, and no new snow had fallen.

Henry shivered.

Brr, it was freezing. He needed more snow, and he needed it fast. His slippers were starting to feel very wet and cold.

Horrid Henry eyed Peter's pathetic lump of snow. Hmmn, thought Horrid Henry.

Hmmn, thought Horrid Henry again.

Well, it's not doing any good sitting there, thought Henry. Someone could trip over it. Someone could hurt themselves. In fact, Peter's snowlump was a danger. He had to act fast before someone fell over it and broke a leg.

Quickly, he scooped up Peter's snowman and stacked it carefully on top of his. Then standing on his tippy toes, he balanced the Abominable Snowman's Viking horns on top.

Da dum!

Much better. And *much* bigger than Margaret's.

Teeth chattering, Horrid Henry sneaked back into his house and crept into bed. Ice cream, here I come, thought Horrid Henry.

Ding dong.

Horrid Henry jumped out of bed. What a morning to oversleep.

Perfect Peter ran and opened the door.

'We're from the Frosty Freeze Ice Cream Factory,' said the man, beaming. 'And you've got the winning snowman out front.'

'I won!' screeched Horrid Henry. 'I won!' He tore down the stairs and out the door. Oh what a lovely lovely day. The sky was blue. The sun was shining — huh???

Horrid Henry looked around.

Horrid Henry's Abominable Snowman was gone.

'Margaret!' screamed Henry. 'I'll kill you!'

But Moody Margaret's snowgirl was gone, too.

The Abominable Snowman's helmet lay on its side on the ground. All that was left of Henry's snowman was . . . Peter's pimple, with its two black stone eyes. A big blue ribbon was pinned to the top.

'But that's *my* snowman,' said Perfect Peter.

'But . . . but . . .' said Horrid Henry.

'You mean, *I* won?' said Peter.

'That's wonderful, Peter,' said Mum.

'That's fantastic, Peter,' said Dad.

'All the others melted,' said the Frosty Freeze man. 'Yours was the only one left. It must have been a giant.'

'It was,' howled Horrid Henry.

HENRY's
Favourite Snowmen

Zombie Snowman

Dracula Snowman

Fangmangler Snowman

PETER's
Favourite Snowmen

Snail Snowman

Bunny Snowman

Worm Snowman

HORRiD HENRY'S
Grump Card

'**I**'ve been so good!' shrieked Horrid Henry.
'Why can't I have a grump card?'
'You have not been good,' said Mum.
'You've been awful,' said Dad.
'No I haven't,' said Henry.

Mum sighed. 'Just today you pinched Peter and called him names. You pushed him off the comfy black chair. You screamed. You wouldn't eat your sprouts. You—'

'Aside from *that*,' said Horrid Henry. 'I've been *so* good. I deserve a grump card.'

'Henry,' said Dad. 'You know we only give grump cards for *exceptionally* good behaviour.'

'But I never get one!' howled Henry.

Mum and Dad looked at each other.

'And why do you think that is?' said Mum.

'Because you're mean and unfair and the worst parents in the world!' screamed Horrid Henry.

What other reason could there be?

A grump card was precious beyond gold and silver and rubies and diamonds. If Mum or Dad thought you'd behaved totally brilliantly above and beyond the call of duty they gave you a grump card. A grump card meant that you could erase any future punishment. A grump card was a glittering, golden, get-out-of-jail-free ticket.

Horrid Henry had never had a grump card. Just think, if he had even one . . . if Dad was in the middle of telling him off, or banning him from the computer for a week, all Henry had to do was hand him a grump card, and, like magic, the telling off would end, the punishment would be erased, and Henry would be back on the computer zapping baddies.

Horrid Henry longed for a grump card. But how could he ever get one? Even Peter, who was always perfect, only had seven. And he'd never even used a single one. What a waste. What a total waste.

Imagine what he could do if he had a grump card . . . He could scoff every sweet and biscuit and treat in the house. He could forget all about homework and watch telly instead. And best of all, if Dad ever tried to ban him from the computer, or Mum shouted that he'd lost his pocket money for a month, all Henry had to do was produce the magic card.

What bliss.

What heaven.

What joy.

But *how* could Henry get a grump card? How? How?

Could he behave totally brilliantly above and beyond the call of duty? Horrid Henry considered. Nah. That was impossible. He'd once spent a whole day being perfect, and even then had ended up being sent to his room.

So how else to get a grump card?

Steal one? Hmmm. Tempting. Very tempting. He could sneak into Peter's room, snatch a grump card or two, then sneak out again. He could even substitute a fake  grump card at the bottom in case Peter noticed his stash was smaller. But then Peter would be sure to tell on him when Henry produced the golden ticket to freedom, and Mum and Dad would be so cross they'd probably *double* his punishment and ban him from the computer for life.

Or, he could kidnap Fluff Puff, Peter's favourite plastic sheep, and hold him for ransom. Yes! And then when Peter  had ransomed him back, Henry could steal him again. And again. Until all Peter's grump cards were his. Yes! He was brilliant. He was a genius. Why had he never thought of this before?

Except . . . if Peter told on him, Henry had a horrible feeling that he would get into trouble. Big big trouble that not even a grump card could get him out of.

Time to think again. Could he swap something for one? What did Henry have that Peter wanted? Comics? No. Crisps? No. Killer Boy Rats CDs? No way.

Henry sighed. Maybe he could *buy* one from Peter. Unfortunately, Horrid Henry never had any money. Whatever pitiful pocket money he ever had always seemed to vanish through his fingers. Besides, who'd want to give that wormy worm a penny?

Better yet, could Henry *trick* Peter into giving him one? Yeah! They could play a great game called *Learn to Share*. Henry could tell Peter to give him half his grump cards as Peter needed to learn to stop being such a selfish hog. It *could* work . . .

There was a snuffling sound, like a pig rustling for truffles, and Perfect Peter stuck his head round the door.

'What are you doing, Henry?' asked Peter.

'None of your business, worm,' said Horrid Henry.

'Want to play with me?' said Peter.

'No,' said Henry. Peter was always nagging Henry to play with him. But when Henry *had* played Robot and Mad Professor with him, for some reason Peter hadn't enjoyed giving Henry all his sweets and money and doing all Henry's chores for him.

'We could play checkers . . . or Scrabble?' said Peter.

'N-O spells no,' said Henry. 'Now get out of—' Horrid Henry paused. Wait a minute. Wait a minute . . .

'How much will you pay me?' said Horrid Henry.

Perfect Peter stared at Henry.

'Pay you? *Pay* you to play with me?'

'Yeah,' said Henry.

Perfect Peter considered.

'How much?' said Peter slowly.

'One pound a minute,' said Henry.

'One pound a minute!' said Peter.

'It's a good offer, toad,' said Henry.

'No it isn't,' said Peter.

'What, you think it should be two pounds a minute?' said Henry. 'Okay.'

'I'm going to tell on you,' said Peter.

'Tell what, worm? That I made you a perfectly good offer? No one's forcing you.'

Perfect Peter paused. Henry was right. He could just say no.

'Or . . .' said Horrid Henry. 'You could pay me in grump cards.'

'Grump cards?' said Peter.

'After all, you have tons and you never use them,' said Henry. 'You could spare one or two or four and never notice . . . and you'll refill your stash in no time.'

It was true that he didn't really need his grump cards, thought Peter. And it would be so nice to play a game . . .

'Okay,' said Peter.

YES! thought Horrid Henry. What a genius he was.

'I charge one grump card a minute.'

'No,' said Peter. 'Grump cards are valuable.'

Horrid Henry sighed.

'Tell you what, because I'm such a nice brother, I will play you a game of Scra . . . Scrab . . .' Horrid Henry could barely bring himself to even say the word *Scrabble* . . . 'for two grump cards. And a game of checkers for two more.'

'And a soft toy tea party?' said Peter.

Did anyone suffer as much as Henry?

He sighed, loudly.

'Okay,' said Horrid Henry. 'But that'll cost you three.'

Horrid Henry stared happily at his seven glorious grump cards. He'd done it! He was free to do anything he wanted. He would be king for ever.

Why wait?

Horrid Henry skipped downstairs, went straight to the sweet jar, and took a huge handful of sweets.

'Put those back, Henry,' said Mum. 'You know sweet day is Saturday.'

'Don't care,' said Henry. 'I want sweets now and I'm having them now.' Shoving the huge handful into his mouth, he reached into the jar for more.

'Henry!' screamed Mum. 'Put those back. That's it. No sweets for a week. Now go straight—'

Horrid Henry whipped
out a grump card and
handed it to Mum.

Mum gasped. Her jaw
dropped.

'Where . . . when . . .
did you get a grump card?'

Henry shrugged. 'I got
it 'cause I was so good.'

Mum stared at him.
Dad must have given him one. How amazing.

Henry strolled into the sitting room. Time for
Terminator Gladiator!

Dad was sitting on the sofa watching the boring
news. Well, not for long. Horrid Henry grabbed the
clicker and switched
channels.

'Hey,' said Dad.
'I was watching.'

'Tough,'
said Henry. 'I'm
watching what I
want to watch. Go
Gladiator!'
he squealed.

'Don't be horrid, Henry. I'm warning you . . .'

Horrid Henry stuck out his tongue at Dad. 'Buzz off, baldie.'

Dad gasped.

'That's it, Henry. No computer games for a week. Now go straight—'

Dad stared at the grump card which Henry waved at him. Henry? A grump card? Mum must have given him one. But how? When?

'I'll just go off now and play on the computer,' said Henry, smirking.

Tee hee. The look on Dad's face. And what fun to play on the computer, after he'd been banned from it! That was well worth a grump card. After all, he had plenty.

Horrid Henry spat his sprouts onto the floor. But a grump card took care of the 'no TV for the rest of the day' punishment. Then he flicked peas at Peter and nicked four of his chips. That was well worth a grump card, too, thought Horrid Henry, to get his pocket money back. Bit of a shame that he had to give two grump cards to lift the ban on going to Ralph's sleepover, but, hey, that's what grump cards were for, right?

'Henry, it's my turn to play on the computer,' said Peter.

'Tough,' said Horrid Henry, zapping and blasting.

'I'm going to tell on you,' said Peter.

'Go ahead,' said Henry. 'See if I care.'

'You're going to get into big, big trouble,' said Peter.

'Go away, wormy worm toady pants poopsicle,' said Henry. 'You're annoying me.'

'Mum! Henry just called me a wormy worm toady pants poopsicle!' shrieked Peter.

'Henry! Stop calling your brother names,' said Mum.

'I didn't,' shouted Henry.

'He did too!' howled Peter.

'Shut up, Ugg-face!' snarled Henry.

'Mum! Henry just called me Ugg-face!'

'That's it,' said Mum. 'Henry! Go to your room. No computer for a—'

Horrid Henry handed over another grump card.

'Henry. Where did you get these?' said Mum.

'I was given them for being good,' said Horrid Henry. That wasn't a lie, because he *had* been good by playing with Peter, and Peter had given them to him.

Perfect Peter burst into tears.

'Henry tricked me,' said Peter. 'He took my grump cards.'

'Didn't.'

'Did.'

'We made a deal, you wibble-face nappy!' shrieked Henry, and attacked. He was a bulldozer flattening a wriggling worm . . .

'AAARRRGGGHH!' screamed Peter.

'You horrid boy,' said Mum. 'No pocket money for a week. No TV for a week. No computer for a week. No sweets for a week. Go to your room!'

Whoa, grump card to the rescue. Thank goodness he'd saved one for emergencies.

What? Huh?

Horrid Henry felt frantically inside his pockets. He looked on the floor. He checked his pockets again.

And again.

There were no grump cards left.

What had he done? Had he just blown all his grump cards in an hour? His precious, precious grump cards? The grump cards he'd never, ever get again?

NOOOOOOOOO!!!!!!!

If I had all the grump cards
I deserve, this would be my grump card heaven.

Eat crisps and chocolate
ALL day

No homework, watch tv

Sit at the computer and
play games

Loads of pocket money

Sneak all the sweets
I can eat

Henry's Top Ten best EVER tricks

1 Scaring the Best Boys Club into giving him all their money by pretending there was a Fangmangler monster in the garden.

2 Telling Peter that a cardboard box was a time machine and making him think he'd travelled to the future.

3 Grabbing everyone's Hallowe'en sweets despite being stuck at home.

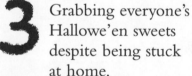

4 Getting rid of Greasy Greta, the Demon Dinner Lady, by putting hot chilli powder in her biscuits.

5 Tricking Bossy Bill into photocopying his bottom.

6 Switching the present tags on Stuck-Up Steve's gifts and his own, so that he got Steve's great gifts and Steve got his horrible ones.

7 Persuading Bossy Bill and Stuck-Up Steve to wear pyjamas for a paintballing party.

8 Escaping from Moody Margaret's school by telling her mum he and Peter had been sick.

9 Terrifying Stuck-Up Steve into thinking there was a monster under his bed.

10 Showing the Bogey Babysitter who's boss by frightening her with a spider in a jar.